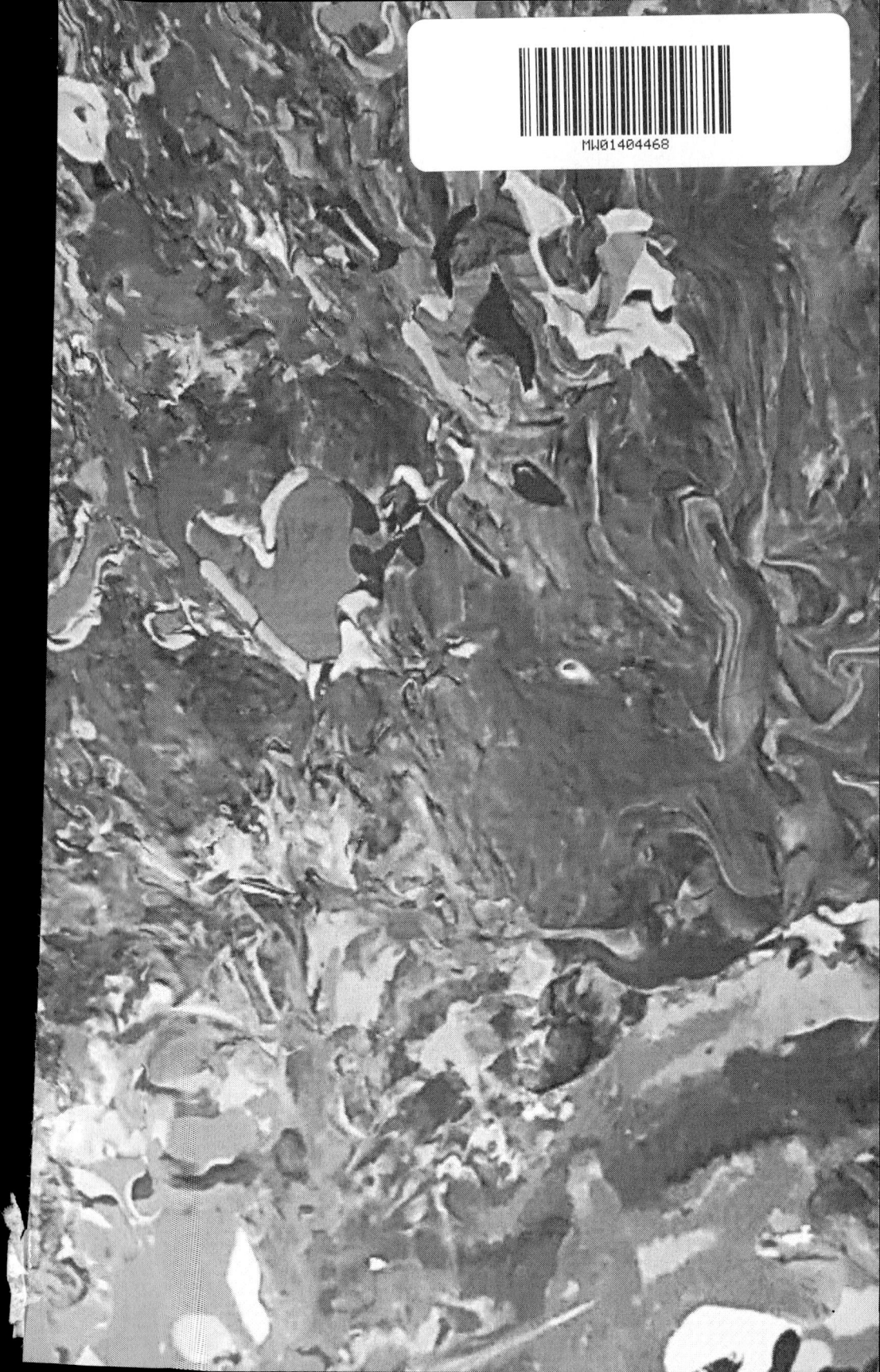

THE POETRY MAN

Rich Osborne

Content and Cover Art

Copyright © 2020, Richard Osborne

All poetry and quotations, unless otherwise noted, Copyright © 2020, Richard Osborne

ISBN - 13

ISBN -10

Disclaimer:

This is a work of fiction, all characters and many places in this book have been generated by the author's imagination and are fictional. Any references made to real places, songs, titles, or persons, are done so for the sole purpose of placing the reader someplace tangible and is not intended to promote those locations or names of those places. The author will not be responsible for any unintentional errors or omissions that may be found or from any consequences resulting from the use of this information.

All rights reserved. No part of this book may be copied or altered in any form or by any means. Brief quotations in a review are allowed.

Published by

Richard Osborne

Email: thepoetryman2020@gmail.com

Dedication

This book is dedicated to all the divine angels here on earth and in heaven who have shown me the greatest gift anyone can give, comes from the heart.

To my wife, Sophie who so unselfishly sacrificed and continues to do so, to gift me and so many others with her love.

To my stepdaughter, Amanda, with whom, I have been honored to have shared so many proud moments, wonderful memories, precious times and laughs along our special journey.

To my grandmother and mom who always believed in me and my gift.

To my dad, for the memorable road trips and adventures we shared.

To Babci, John and Uncle Pete though I never met you personally, I feel your love, guidance and presence every day.

To the "Bomba" girls and their families, thank you for your love and support.

And to the people, places and experiences that have come into my life over the years, and the memories made that I will forever cherish.

Contents

Contents

Goodbye Thirty-Four Park Street 16

The Voices Begin 24

The Journey to The West Coast 29

The Land of Poetic Dreams 35

"Pops" 44

Seagulls and Greeting Cards 49

Pleasant Bluffs Drive 58

Moss Colored Carpet 65

Missing Piece of The Puzzle 75

The Plymouth Rock Inn 80

A Mentor and A Teacher 91

Inspiration 100

The First Kiss 108

Return to Sender 116

Freelancing 123

Moving On 129

The Earrings and The Crystal Angel 136

Pampering 144

You Make Me Feel Brand New	154
Jade and Romance	167
The English Countryside	174
The Journal and The Painting	191
"You Are So Beautiful, To Me"	198
McCovey's Cove	207
Shells, Sea Glass, Stones and Driftwood	214
The Children Make an Impact	221
Emerald Eyes and Promises	228
Unwrapping the Surprise	240
101 Hearts	248
The Connection	257
Manning Osborne of Kingstanding	264
Novella	272
Vineyard Wedding	278
Weekend in Victoria	286
Conclusion	293
About the Author	299

Introduction

How Could Love Be So Perfect

Life was so perfect from day one for Michael and Felicia. One could only wonder how. I guess as we age, we become more adaptive, accommodating and accepting of the things that used to turn our world inside out. Take for instance, our pasts, we could live in them or move on. In the case of Michael and Felicia, they moved on.

Felicia dealt with the death of her husband, Michael the ending of his marriage. Yes, it took Felicia some time to open herself up to love again but, she did and all under the perfect of circumstances.

For her and Michael, it was treading slowly and building a strong friendship based on respect, trust and forgiveness. Forgiveness for them wasn't about saying, "I am sorry for what I have done". Forgiveness for them was about being able to respect where each had been and trust and embrace without question, who they were as individuals.

Michael never felt insecure with Felicia. As beautiful as she was and as successful as she was, he knew she could be with anyone she chose but, had chosen him. Felicia always made it clear to Michael that she was completely happy having him in her life and it showed in everything she did.

Felicia Stouffer accepted everything about Michael Langston. She often told him how she admired the fact that he had given up a life of complacency to pursue his true calling in life. She knew he was willing to do whatever he had to, to make his dream of writing a book, a reality. Even if it meant starting all over again.

Their beliefs and teachings about what is needed to sustain a long term, successful relationship meshed from the get go. Although, they may not have spoken about it in the initial stages it was ingrained in the two of them. That is why the physical plane they travelled was able to reach unlimited heights of oneness. Yes, it was probably difficult given the attraction they both felt for one another, to abstain. They did and as a result of that, when they made love for the first time, it was out of pure love not, physical lust. The love they grew to share, was an inclusion of all they believed in as individuals now joined as a couple.

Chapter 1

Goodbye Thirty-Four Park Street

Goodbye Thirty-Four Park Street

It was another cold and dreary February day in Newark, New Jersey. I'd awakened at four twenty-eight, before the sun to make sure I gave myself enough time to get ready for my long journey to the West Coast.

As I dressed, I kept looking into the cherry rimmed, oval mirror at Melanie who was still sound asleep, warmed by the quilt my grandmother had made for us as a wedding present. As I buttoned my shirt, I kept looking to see if my sleeping beauty would arise to share a warm cup of coffee as she had done for the past ten years.

It was a ritual with us to have some precious moments together before I left for work. I would get up around five and walk over to the plaza for bagels and the paper. When I got back to the apartment, Melanie would have a fresh pot of coffee ready. We would embrace in celebration of a brand, new day, carrying on like little kids, laughing and hugging as we danced across the kitchen floor while the mellow saxophone sounds of, "Blue and Sentimental" filled the room.

My train usually left around six-thirty, this gave us an hour before I had to go. Melanie always walked down with me to the front porch where we would embrace until we heard the train's whistle blow. This morning was different from all the others and I knew in my heart there was nothing I could do to change that. Suitcase in hand, I looked around once again to the small, cozy apartment that had been home for ten years.

Michael glanced over to the side of the bed where Melanie was wrapped in dreams. He kissed her softly on the lips, turned towards the hall and closed the door with a quiet whisper behind him.

As the brown and white taxi pulled up, he stood on the wet lawn and looked back up to the 3rd floor window. The curtains were pulled slightly. Melanie stood in the window. Michael could see tears falling from her soft emerald eyes.

He wanted so desperately to run back upstairs and hold her. In his heart, he knew he had to turn away.

As he opened the door to the taxi, Michael heard Melanie calling out his name.

"Michael, wait, please wait. Don't go yet, I need to hold you once more." He put his suitcase down and ran to her open arms.

As they stood there on the porch just gazing into each other's swollen eyes, the tears began to fall. Michael pulled Melanie close to him and began to speak.

"It all seems like a dream. I keep thinking I am just getting on the train and will be home tonight like always." He looked into her eyes again as he spoke.

"Melanie, I know you may never understand me. As much as I feel love for you, I can't see me being able to give you what you truly want from life and that is a family. It has been a painful battle with me to try and accept that, but I can no longer fight the reality of what I am feeling inside. You will find the one who makes your life complete, I know now that I am not that person".

He continued to hold her as he spoke.

"I always thought I was complete with you, but I want more out of life than just surviving in this crazy world. I cannot explain it but there is this calling, a spiritual message I keep hearing over and over in my head. It has been going on for some time now and as much as I try to fight it, it just gets stronger. "

As our lips met, Melanie pulled me close to her and in a soft voice began to tell me her thoughts. "Michael, I know you need to do this and that is why I am crying. I want you to find your dreams not hold you back. I have watched you toss and turn at night and felt you fighting this calling for so long and I too feel like this is the time for you to go. I am not certain what our future holds and will let it unfold the way it is supposed to. Know that I will always be just a phone call away if you need me for anything".

Melanie kissed Michael one last time before they broke away from one another.

As the cab pulled away from thirty-four Park Street, Michael looked up. The curtain was still parted but the window was now empty.

The drive down the Garden State Parkway to the airport had Michael deep in thought. His years with Melanie and been filled with so many beautiful memories. He thought about the time ten years ago, he had surprised her with tickets to a Bruce Springsteen concert. Michael then recalled the first time he met Melanie's parents.

Antonio and Maria Basilica were born in Italy. They had immigrated to America to build a life for themselves when they were in their late twenties. Through the years Michael would sit at the table with his father-in law and hear stories about the man's childhood in a small Sicilian village, San

Cataldo. There was always a bottle of Antonio's homemade wine on the table. The two of them would savor the wine and the stories would begin to unfold.

Antonio had tried several vocations upon arriving in the United States, but it was the restaurant business that enabled him to create a wealth he could not obtain in any other venture. Every minute of the day he put in brought him closer to retirement where he could truly enjoy all his years of hard work. He would often remark that the younger generation had no ambition and were afraid of hard work.

"The American way has changed so much in the last forty years, he would huff. We did what we had to do, they were no hand-outs, we just worked hard day in and day out." Five years earlier, Antonio told his family they were going into the restaurant business. He said he would need his wife and daughter by his side if it was going to be successful.

Those work ethics were never more evident than at Basil's. The restaurant drew a large following because of his cooking and family atmosphere. Melanie left her job at the small café where she and Michael first fell for one another to help with the family business. Michael Langston and Melanie Basilica were two different people from very different backgrounds. She had come from a strong, close-knit Italian family. Michael's parents divorced when he was two years old. Being without any real guidance from such an early age, Michael had an inner sense he had to figure things out on his own. As a young boy he was curious, always wanting to know why things were the way they were. As he got older, he began answering his own questions by reading and exploring. This is where the contrast came in for the two of them.

Melanie lived by what she saw, Michael lived trying to learn what he didn't know. Often Michael's need to find answers would lead him astray.

When he and Melanie first met, he was like a stray puppy. He had never really settled down. Michael's biggest battle was his restlessness.

As much as Melanie adored and loved him, Michael's ever-changing ways would constantly test her sanity.

After ten years together, Michael realized he was being unfair by expecting the love of his life to alter her way of life for him. As admirable as he felt about Melanie's parent's ability to accept one another's differences and build a lifetime together till death did them part, Michael had a hard time seeing how long-lasting relationships work. "Maybe", he thought to himself, "That voice was there all along trying to tell him, but he fought it to try and conform to a way of life he never knew.

The constant battle within finally brought Michael to the conclusion he could no longer settle for a life trying to be someone he knew deep in his heart he wasn't. When he concluded that it was time for him to leave the life, he had grown accustomed to over the last decade to pursue his dream of writing, the love he once had for Melanie was separated by the realization that he had no choice but to let go.

The night before he left for San Francisco, Michael went to Basil's as they were closing and sat down to talk to Antonio and Maria about his plans. As the three of them sat talking, the phone rang. Maria excused herself and strode to the kitchen to answer it. On the other end was Melanie.

Michael never knew it was her calling to tell her mom what was transpiring with him. She told her mother she had come to accept it and she and her dad should not try to deter Michael from following his dream.

Chapter 2

The Voices Begin

The Voices Begin

Michael spent eight years on Vancouver Island in the city of Victoria, the capital of the Province of British Columbia. In 1970, at the tender age of fifteen, his mom decided it was time to pack it all in and make the move across country to be closer to her family.

Michael recalls his first memories of that beautiful place.

The morning after we arrived, my cousin and I got on bicycles and headed out from my Aunt's house towards Ogden Point, to go fishing off the breakwater.

The sun was creeping up from the East as we made our way past the mist covered knoll that led up to the old Checkerboard House on Dallas Road. As we peddled through Beacon Hill Park, there was an incredible fresh chill sweeping across my cheeks. I turned to my left to see where the brisk air was coming from. As I looked beyond the weeping branches of an aged willow, my eyes caught a glimpse of a magnificent sight. I pushed down on my pedals as hard as I could, bouncing up over the curb and across the wind-swept grass to the shoreline. I pulled my bike closer to the rugged edge of Horseshoe Bay and rested at the cliff's edge to get a closer look.

The blue-gray waters rolled between the coastline of Port Angeles, Washington to the island's beaches. I pulled myself to the edge of the sweeping grass and looked down.

As each wave washed upon the shore, the stones that were left behind appeared to have been polished by the gentle brushing of the ocean's sand.

I laid my bike down upon the grass and ran down a steep path to embrace the miracle I was witnessing.

As the next wave gently washed upon the sand, I reached down and scooped up a handful of the polished gems. I carried my shimmering treasure over to the cliff side, eased myself onto a piece of driftwood and leaned against the soft stilts of grass that grew out from the sandy cliff.

I sat there for what seemed to be hours and just stared across the water.

The site that held me was the Cascade Mountains arching up through the morning clouds, across that blue-gray sea.

I turned my head up towards the sky and caught sight of something in flight, flashing across the early light's dawning. It was a sight that would change my life forever.

It was in that moment, I saw the vision.

In that moment, my destiny on this earth became a reality, a destiny I struggled hard to recapture for many years.

I remember it like it was yesterday.

I can still feel the beat of my heart and the breath that expelled itself from inside as I focused all my energy on the gracefulness of that lone seagull.

His feathers bore a glistening light that streaked across the sky creating a trail of golden white hues. As I fixed my eyes upon him, he seemed to feel my presence for as far away from me he could have chosen to fly, he turned his beak downward and glided as if suspended in time, towards me. He landed at my outstretched feet, lifted his head and looked into my eyes.

Michael felt something reverberating inside. In the silence and encounter of that moment, the words, "Behold the beauty before you and let it resonate in your heart. You have been given a gift to capture God's beauty in words. You are, The Poetry Man."

Was it his imagination, or had the time finally come for Michael to stop looking outwards to find himself?

The gull turned towards the water and ascended into the heavens.

Michael just laid there and followed the gulls flight beyond the farthest cloud. He felt something magical transpiring inside of him. It was as if the world outside of his physical being had become a doorway to eternal life and his internal being was a transmitter of poetic messages capable of healing through imagery.

Michael had been writing poetry since he was eight years old. As he got older, he began to question his uncanny ability to put words together. Now he began to understand.

He reflected upon all the things he had written over his young life.

"I never had to think about what I was going to write, I would just feel it. Now, I see the message more clearly. All I have to do is believe what I feel inside, let go and let the transmitter take over."

He thought back to his encounter with that gull once again as he rose up from his driftwood bed and brushed the sand off. It was as if a voice from somewhere in time had been channeled through this gull.

As much as Michael wanted to share his enlightening experience he felt, at the age of fifteen, encounters like this aren't considered normal and if shared with others he may wind up in long term therapy. He smiled to himself as he walked back up the cliff to retrieve his bike.

"So, I guess I am, The Poetry Man." He liked the sound of that!

Chapter 3

The Journey to The West Coast

The Journey to The West Coast

For the first time in over ten years, Michael Langston was travelling without Melanie.

Flight 917 was boarding at Gate 10. Michael looked out the windows lining the long corridor as he approached the metal detector. The morning mist trickled down the plates of glass.

It was another cold and dreary February day in the city.

In six hours, Michael would be away from the Northeast metro area and setting his feet upon the ground to start a new life in San Francisco.

Michael stared out his window and watched the clouds envelope the silver wings. As he cast his eyes out into the morning skies, he felt the tears fall as he recalled all the good times Melanie and he had shared. His thoughts were politely broken by a soft voice. Michael captures what transpired next.

I turned to look, and my eyes met one of the most beautiful smiles I'd seen in a while. This woman saw my tears, apologized for bothering me and turned towards the seat that was open across the aisle.

"It's okay, you are welcome to sit here, I was just reminiscing some wonderful memories." Michael said as he dried his eyes.

She eased herself down next to me extended her well-manicured hand to introduce herself. "Hi, my name is Felicia Stouffer. Michael extended his hand and responded. I am Michael Langston.

"Please don't feel uncomfortable, I kind of understand the feeling. I was there emotionally not too long ago." Felicia said as she smiled at me with a warm expression on her face and I began to feel comfortable knowing Felicia would be my flight mate for the trip.

She reached into her briefcase and handed me a tissue all the time looking at me as if to ease my pain.

Her eyes were a beautiful emerald green color. *"Just like Melanie's."* Michael thought to himself. He couldn't help but tell her how she reminded him of the woman he had just said goodbye to a few hours ago.

"There is only one person whose eyes radiate such beauty. Melanie and I were together for ten years and I never knew God had given anyone else those emerald green eyes."

Felicia's face at first glowed hearing Michael's compliment but began to lose a bit of its sparkle as she spoke. "Michael, it's funny how much you also remind me of the man I was with for sixteen years. I saw you getting on the plane and my heart just stopped." Michael was fully focused on every word Felicia was saying.

"He told me that night he was leaving for England the next day to take care of a family emergency. Adrian's grandmother had taken ill, and he wanted to be with her; that was the last I ever saw of him."

Felicia stared past Michael out the window. "Adrian called when he landed in London and again after he got to the hospital. He said when he arrived at her bedside, his grandmother was in her final stages of life. He did say that she had opened her eyes when she heard his voice and smiled at him."

"The last words she spoke," Adrian said, his voice cracking, were ones she had read from Shakespeare when he was a child. "Parting is such sweet sorrow. Until we meet again." He said she closed her eyes and had the most beautiful smile on her face. I knew Adrian was very distraught over her death. She had raised him from a child and returned to her homeland when Adrian and I married". Felicia's voice was almost a whisper. "I never knew he would end his life over it." She went on. "The phone rang the following night, as soon as I heard the tone in Benjamin's voice, I knew something was wrong."

Benjamin Stillwater was the CEO of Randall Publishing House where Adrian had started as a Copywriter after graduating from Columbia. Ben had guided Adrian through the ranks, and they had become the best of friends.

"We were at Ben's house on New Year's Eve when he announced he was stepping down as CEO and had chosen Adrian to succeed him." Felicia began recalling the conversation with Adrian's boss as Michael eased deeper into his seat. "He took his own life that night when he got back to the hotel. Housekeeping found a bottle of sleeping pills and whiskey by his side. I am so sorry and shocked over this Felicia. There was nothing anyone could do." Ben said, his voice trailing off as he ended the conversation.

"Felicia, my life did not suffer the tragedy yours did. I will be okay."

They talked throughout lunch.

Michael shared his reason for being on that flight.

"I am going to San Francisco to begin a new life, one that will let me focus on my dream of being an author. I had a very comfortable life in New Jersey, but it just didn't feel complete. I had a calling when I was fifteen that began to resurface a few years ago. Working in New York City was tearing me down."

Michael leaned closer to Felicia. "I was afraid to tell anyone about the voice I heard on the beach that day because they would have thought I was crazy. Truth is, I was killing myself trying to conform to a way of life that was not me. That is when the voice told me. "Behold the beauty before you and let it resonate in your heart. You have been given a gift to capture God's beauty in words.

"Felicia, do you think I am nuts?"

"Not at all Michael, not at all."

Michael stared out the window one last time before drawing the shade to watch the movie. He liked to look out at the clouds as the sun's light swept across the horizon. He had flown many times before but had never seen a sky as beautiful as this. Michael glanced back at Felicia, her eyes were affixed to the screen. As he pulled the shade down, a sparkle caught the corner of his eye. He moved closer to the window thinking it must be, a reflection of sunlight from another aircraft's wing in the distant. Then he remembered the gull. "Ah, the messenger that landed at his outstretched feet," he thought to himself.

Then he heard a quiet whisper echoing the words once again.

"Behold the beauty before you and let it resonate in your heart. You have been given a gift to capture God's beauty in words. You are, The Poetry Man."

Chapter 4

The Land of Poetic Dreams

The Land of Poetic Dreams

Michael brushed Felicia's shoulder softy. "We are here, in the land of poetic dreams. Look there's the Golden Gate Bridge." The tall orange arches of the bridge were reaching high above the glistening waters of the San Francisco Bay. Beneath the architectural landmark stood the Island of Alcatraz, the infamous prison that housed many of the twentieth centuries' most notorious criminals.

The planes wheels made a screeching sound as it skimmed the runway. The nose of the plane came down on to the dry tarmac. As they began to taxi towards the terminal, Felicia reached into her purse and handed Michael her business card and said. "If you need a place to stay until you get on your feet, please let me offer that to you. I have more room than I need. It would be nice to have my "new" friend in my life besides it's cheaper than a hotel and apartments are very expensive in the Bay area."

As his fingers glossed over the black embossed lettering, Michael began to ponder Felicia's proposal. He looked up at Felicia and spoke. "I truly appreciate your offer. It would give me a chance to get re-acclimated with the city, find a job and look for my own place. I can accept your offer but for no longer than two months, fair enough?"

Felicia looked at Michael and smiled. "Of course, Michael, it will all work out just fine for you, you have determination, faith and believe in yourself, I can sense it and see it in you."

Michael held the card up and ran his fingers over the black lettering once again:

Felicia Stouffer
21st Century Advertising
San Francisco, Ca.

The card was nothing fancy or overdone, classy, just like the woman sitting next to him.

The plane came to a soft stop at the terminal.

As we were getting ready to disembark, Felicia nudged me.

"Michael, I really had a wonderful time flying with you, you are a special soul. Funny how, in just five and a half hours I feel like I have known you a lifetime. For some reason, I do feel like we have met somewhere before, maybe another life?"

"I agree Felicia, seems our lives were destined to come together today."

Felicia and Michael walked towards the baggage claim area, her hand securely tucked under his arm. They strode along the terminal opting to walk instead of getting on the moving passenger belt.

It was a bright, sunny day. The sun was peering through the glass as the two made their way towards the baggage carousel.

As they approached, Felicia looked over at a young girl holding her mother's hand. She couldn't have been more than five, blonde curly locks and big blue eyes.

Felicia stopped to admire the young lady. "Oh, Michael, isn't she just gorgeous?" "Adrian and I were planning to start a family as soon as he got back from England. I guess God had other plans."

"I know the feeling, Melanie and I talked about having children too I just never felt ready."

"Do you think you might go for it someday Michael? Felicia asked. "Feel settled enough with yourself to allow a child into your world?"

"I can't really answer that right now. My focus and energy are probably so wrapped up in getting my life on track, writing my book, seeing if this is what has been keeping me reaching for that star. One thing I have come to know, and it was in that voice I heard. We spend our life looking outward trying to grasp something externally, that voice was my calling to look inside, feel what is in my heart."

Felicia stopped and looked directly into Michael's eyes.

"Michael, that is so simple yet, profound, I completely understand how people get caught up chasing a dream outside of who they are as a person."

Felicia began waving over the throngs of travelers waiting for their luggage. "Cal, I'm over here."

Michael looked over by the carousel. The man she was calling to was tanned and well over six feet tall. "*My Goodness*," Michael thought to himself. "*This guy is built like a linebacker.*"

Felicia watched Michael stop in his tracks when he saw her driver and smiled. "Gentle as a puppy, Michael. Cal has been through a lot in life and I assure you, if I am comfortable enough to bring you into my life, he knows me and has already accepted you." Felicia was right.

As the two approached Cal he began to smile as he noticed Felicia's arm tucked under Michaels.

"Welcome home Ms. Stouffer, I see you've met a new friend." Cal said in a deep voice that matched his awesome size.

"Cal," meet Michael. "We met on the plane and something just connected. You know I haven't really felt comfortable with too many people since Adrian's death but somehow Michael was able to bring a sense of ease and comfort out in me." Felicia told Cal as she looked up at him with a warm smile.

Michael reached out his hand to greet Cal. "I think I am the lucky one. I was the one leaving a world of certainty for one that was unknown, and Felicia just happened to come along and put a sense of calm in me. I am so glad I asked her to sit with me or I would probably be wandering around here like a lost soul." Cal placed his other hand on top of Michaels looked him square in the eyes and gleamed. As his huge hands enfolded around his, Michael could feel the warmth and gentleness Felicia described.

Cal stood on one side of me, Felicia on the other as we waited for our luggage to surface.

I had my one bag, all I cared to take, just enough to get me started with my new life. I knew whatever else I needed I could pick up in San Francisco. Whenever Melanie and I travelled, she would over pack and never use half of what she brought. I would wind up lugging three to four suitcases and a backpack. To say the least, it was quite cumbersome dragging those suitcases around.

Felicia was a seasoned and consummate traveler. She knew how to make the most of her wardrobe and personal necessities. Both our bags arrived. Cal took hers and offered to take mine. I looked at him and laughed. "Thanks, but I think will be able to manage this."

Felicia informed Cal she had extended an invitation to Michael to stay at the house until he got his feet on the ground.

"I am totally okay with that Ms. Stouffer. As, long as, it works for you, it works for me."

As they walked towards the parking garage, Cal engaged Michael in conversation.

'I know quite a bit about the area and am happy to help in any way I can. Any friend of Felicia's is a friend of mine. I have some friends who live in the city. As soon as the colleges are out, I am certain something will become available.

"Thanks Cal, I feel at home already," Michael responded.

Michael had been to San Francisco before. Although it had been quite some time ago, he still remembered the layout of the city. He had ventured to Fisherman's Wharf, Chinatown, Lombard Street and of course remembered the ride on the famous trolleys. A friend of his had relocated from New Jersey to Oakland with his company. He and his wife invited Michael to come visit them. Michael would be in Vancouver and had his flight rerouted so he could spend three days with them. He had quite the time taking in an Oakland A's game and savoring Peking duck in Chinatown.

As they approached the silver Land Rover, Cal leaned over to Michael while popping open the trunk. "I know Felicia will enjoy your company right now, she's gone through some tough times lately. I know Adrian has been on her mind and she just hasn't been herself lately. Seeing her with you is the first time I have seen her smiling in a long time."

"It's funny," Cal continued. "When I saw you walking towards me in the airport, I had to do a double take. You do resemble Adrian in many ways."

Michael smiled as he handed Cal his bag and stepped into the Rover.

"Cal, can you please stop by my office before we head home?"

"Of course, Ms. Stouffer." Cal replied.

As the three sped off towards the heart of San Francisco, Felicia reached over and took Michael's hand. "Thank you, I know you are going to have a great time here. Thanks for making me smile again."

As they made their way out of the airport, Michael caught Cal looking into the rearview mirror. There was a look of contentment on his face.

The Rover made its way through the city and pulled alongside the curb that was now bustling with pedestrians. As the vehicle came to a halt, Michael rolled down his window and looked up to capture the gleaming magnificence of the steel structure.

As he has done for the past four years, Cal got out and walked over to the curb to open the door for Felicia. "What time would you like me to pick you up Ms. Stouffer?" Cal asked.

"It's 4:28 now let's say 6:30, that will give me enough time to look over my mail, check my messages and give everyone the good news about the Adams Apparel account."

Michael got out to escort Felicia to the front door. They exchanged a polite hug and bid a brief farewell. As Cal and Michael headed out into traffic,

Felicia strolled into the lobby of the building that housed the offices of 21st Century Advertising.

Chapter 5

"Pops"

"Pops"

"Good afternoon, Ms. Stouffer." a blue-capped doorman called as Felicia strode past the security desk towards the elevator. "So nice to see such a radiant smile of beauty." The gent remarked.

Jerry Bristol had been a doorman since the day the building first opened its doors in 1994. He had seen many beautiful women come and go through his lobby, but none had made an impression on him as Felicia Stouffer. The tall and lanky white-haired Englishman always had a kind remark for the hundreds of people that passed through his doors each day but, he saved the best compliments for Felicia.

Jerry had immigrated from Liverpool, England. He settled in New York City where he became a cherished cornerstone with his crisp accent at the Park Place Hotel in Manhattan.

Bristol remained with the New York hotel for almost thirty years and still recalls the day the citizens of New York came out in droves to surprise him with a farewell party.

Jerry never married and found himself in the city of San Francisco shortly thereafter.

His reputation followed him to the Bay area. A job as Head Captain awaited him when he arrived. Jason Congdon, a wealthy New York real estate developer knew just who he wanted manning his prized possession when he entered the doors to his new building.

At the ripe young age of sixty-five, Jerry was affectionately called, "Pops" by the forty-two old financier.

Jason had always marveled at Bristol's ability to handle himself with the utmost dignity no matter who walked through his doors. He had confided in Jerry about his own father over the years. He often mentioned how he wished his own father had taken him under his wings like "Pops" had done.

Jason Congdon was twelve years old when his dad slipped Jerry one hundred dollars and told the new doorman to take his kid to a ballgame since he was too busy to do so himself. There were many ballgames after that as well as circuses, parades and other things a father takes pride in sharing with his son growing up.

Joshua Congdon had everything anyone could ever ask for except the time to watch his son grow into a man. The younger Congdon realized this a long time ago and through the years felt he owed everything he had become to Jerry Bristol.

He couldn't think of a better way to honor, "Pops" than to name his new building, "**The Bristol Building**."

"I'll never forget the first day I reported to my new job," Jerry recalled. "There were dignitaries all dressed up in tuxedos and gowns. It was like one of those Hollywood motion picture premiers. As I walked up the steps, Jason ran up to me, put his arm around me and said. "I've got a big surprise for you."

He reached into his pocket and pulled out a big golden key with the name, Bristol engraved on its face. He put his arm over my shoulder and led me up the new steps to the shiny steel and glass doors. As we approached the entrance Jason reached over and handed Jerry a pair of scissors.

"Pops," he said with tears forming at the corners of his dark blue eyes. "I couldn't have done it without you." He pulled Jerry back towards the steps and turned him to face the glistening silver cornerstone. Jason whispered in Jerry's ears, "You have given me so much, this is something I had always dreamed I could do to show you just how much you have meant to me ever since that first ballgame. My own father never got to see just how far that hundred dollars went that day."

<u>ERECTED ON THIS SITE</u>
<u>JULY 20,1994</u>
<u>THE BRISTOL BUILDING</u>
<u>NAMED FOR JERRY BRISTOL</u>
<u>A CORNERSTONE OF HUMANITY</u>
<u>TO ALL WHO PASS THROUGH THESE DOORS</u>

Chapter 6

Seagulls and Greeting Cards

Seagulls and Greeting Cards

Felicia stood in front of the elevator waiting to be taken up to the forty-second floor. All around her was the hustle and bustle of people heading home after a full day in the office. Felicia's day would end in a couple of hours.

The bell rang and the elevator doors opened wide. Riders stepped off the shiny steel carriage that transported them swiftly up and down the floors of the Bristol Building. As Felicia poked her head in to make sure the car was empty, a petite young lady fumbled past her., stopped, and turned around almost dizzily, exclaiming, "Felicia, I didn't expect you until Monday."

Felicia looked over her shoulder at the little redhead. "You know me Jackie, I can't stay away for too long. Anyway, come back upstairs with me for a few minutes okay?"

The two ladies boarded the elevator. Jackie pushed the button for the forty second floor. The doors shut tightly, and the elevator started to ascend.

"So boss, how did it go in "The Big Apple?" Felicia's assistant asked excitedly.

"That's exactly why I came in. I couldn't wait until Monday to share the big news. Tracey Adams signed us on to launch their new apparel line.

Jackie gave Felicia a big hug.

"We're talking thirty-five million, sweetheart." Felicia beamed.

"My goodness woman, how'd you do it?" Jackie giggled.

"I just told Mr. Adams there wasn't a tighter, more creative and ingenious family in the advertising business than the one here in San Francisco." As the doors opened to the offices of 21st Century Advertising, Felicia leaned over to Jackie winked and said. "I made him an offer he couldn't refuse!"

Felicia was now exuding the confidence that carried her from a small one room studio adjacent to Fisherman's Wharf to the top floor of one of San Francisco's most prestigious buildings. As Felicia spoke, Jackie was seeing something she hadn't seen in her boss in a while.

"Felicia, this account has really put some sunshine back in your life, hasn't it?"

Felicia glanced over, her emerald eyes gleaming. "Let's just say, it was a wonderful, wonderful trip."

Dressed exquisitely as always, Felicia strode through the office with a graceful, yet relaxed air about herself stopping to exchange hugs and share the wonderful news with her employees.

21st Century Advertising was like one big happy family. The sign outside Felicia's office read:

"My door is always open and so is my heart"

This message was what her agency was all about.

Things weren't always easy for the ad executive. In the beginning she struggled to keep her head above water in a market that was very cut throat. Not what you knew but who you knew!

From New York to Los Angeles, she faced stiff competition. Felicia Stouffer won because of her uncanny ability to recognize the real needs of people. Instead of going for glitz and trends, Felicia reached out to touch the emotional side of advertising.

She started her own business with the $10,000 gift her father had given her when she graduated from college.

Felicia designed her own line of greeting cards. She used the poetry she had written in high school to launch her career. Unlike the large commercial card companies where every word had to rhyme, Felicia wrote what she felt others really wanted to say from their heart. Because of this approach, she was able to carve out her own niche in the greeting card market.

In an article written about Felicia in, "<u>Women Leaders in Business</u>", two of her prized mementos, a framed writer's test she had taken for Hallmark when she was sixteen and a poem entitled, <u>Wind Swept Sea</u>, she had purchased in a small book store on Vancouver Island, before she left for college were mentioned.

When asked about Hallmark, Felicia laughed when she recalled the fifty-eight pages writer's test. "I never did send it in, it just seemed too "in the box", for how I express myself. I envisioned a pool of writers sitting at their desks with a Thesaurus looking for words to rhyme with, "*birthday*."

In her office next to the great window that overlooks the bay, framed in light oak on yellow parchment paper is the poem hand written in calligraphy.

Wind swept sea,

Sand castles and memories.

So much I have seen thorough these pale blue skies,

I often wonder, if only, I could fly.

Far away lies the end, a still, quiet mystery,

Horizons begin there where my eyes meet the sea.

*A grain of sand where once stood a sand castle,
It's all in the wind now, it's all in the wind now.
Written by: The Poetry Man*

When asked where her inspiration at such a young age came from, Felicia shared her story about her life before coming to San Francisco.

"When I look at the poem, it reminds me of growing up in Oak Bay, on Vancouver Island. I would spend my days on the beach watching the seagulls glide over the ocean. I always dreamed of being able to fly. There I was looking at the gulls in flight thinking, "If only I had your wings." Ironic, I would find that poem. I often wondered who really wrote it and why they didn't sign it with their real name. One day, I will.

"I go back there every chance I get to unwind and write." She told the interviewer.

"Why did you ever leave such an inspirational place?"

"I left the island to attend college in Washington State and headed south after graduation where I discovered San Francisco. I'd never seen a city as beautiful as Victoria until I came to the bay area. I was never fond of big cities, but San Francisco was a haven for creative people. It was like stepping back in time with the cable cars and, the wharf with the gulls flying all around, it was heaven to me." Felicia glowed as she reminisced how it all started. "That is where I had my first studio, a thirty by thirty storefront down on the wharf."

She went on with her story. "I would sit on a bench by the dock every day for lunch and feed the gulls. "When I leave my office now and need to get lost, that is where you will find me."

When asked about her success, Felicia told the magazine. "It was only when I followed my heart that I realized anything I set my mind on was possible."

"I have always believed we are all born with a special talent to succeed with in this world and if we could find that one gift and use it for doing good in this world, we will prosper. Too many people let fear stand in their way. They never realize their full potential because they are too busy doing what everyone else thinks they should do." Felicia paused, then went on. "There is no real easy way of getting there, sometimes you may feel you have been dealt a lousy hand, so you just give up and fold. I can't really say what has made me persevere except that I have always believed in my dreams no matter what others said. If you were to ask people who knew me growing up what they thought, they would simply say, she was a dreamer, that I was." Felicia said nodding her head up and down.

"Any advice for someone trying to get into the world of advertising?" The interviewer inquired.

"I try to tell the young people I meet today that no dream is ever too far from achieving if they truly believe in themselves, that in my opinion is the key, believe in yourself. I have been fortunate to find and surround myself with the right people, the ones who have dreams. My job I believe is to encourage the free spirit of thinking, to ease those boundaries that seem to confine most of us. Whether others think I am a philosophical thinker or not doesn't really matter. I give the people who work for 21st Century the freedom to express their wildest imaginations." The interviewer continued writing as Felicia spoke.

"I hope that I can guide them in the right direction through my examples of dedication and hard work and rewards. The world of advertising is a fierce and competitive one, my people know and respect that." Felicia strode over to the window. "With all my successes, I have never lost sight of the human element and that is why I do not fear being swept under. If one day I walked in here and felt as if I had to approach my job any different than I do, I would pack it all in and go back to my little studio."

The article was published and received rave reviews not only from women all over the country who supported Felicia's courage to do things on her own terms but also from many men who felt they had lost touch with what real success in life was all about.

A famous CEO from a Fortune 50 company had written to Felicia after reading the article to thank her for opening his eyes not only to the human elements of business but, to the human side of himself. It was a letter she cherished. She would never display it amongst the other mementos. The letter read...

Dear Ms. Stouffer,

The hardest part I had in writing this letter was the heading. While I am so accustomed to addressing all my correspondence in a congenial and professional manner, this one time I felt the urge to just write and say, "Dear Felicia," Your article touched me. It opened my eyes beyond any horizon I had set sail upon in my sixty-seven years in business and my eighty-nine years in this life. I began to feel like Ebenezer in that famous Christmas tale. With each word of your article, I was taken through my past, to my present and even into my future. As I read each word, I realized how blind I had been all these years to the true meaning of success.

I lay in my bed now. There are no more certainties in my life. All the material successes I have had cannot buy me one single second of time beyond that which I have been allotted. The words you have spoken, I hold close to my heart. Those words are my salvation. Felicia, if I may call you that, thank you for enriching this stubborn, old life. Thank you for putting a smile of hope on this wrinkled face. Let all who read your words take the time to understand as you have done so well, that we must take the time to believe in and pursue our dreams or forever fail our destiny and lifetime in this world.

Respectfully Yours,

J.P. Rickens

While there was a certain pride in showing the letter and person from whom it had come, Felicia chose to keep it as a personal memento.

Chapter 7

Pleasant Bluffs Drive

Pleasant Bluffs Drive

It was now 6:20. Felicia had filled everyone in on the news, taken care of her mail and other correspondence. She scrambled to get her things together so she could be downstairs in time to meet Cal and Michael.

The rest of the family at the agency had already gone home. Felicia locked up the office and walked briskly towards the elevator. She exuded an energy she hadn't felt in a long time. The bell rang and the elevator doors sprung open. As she stepped in, Felicia glanced into the mirrored wall adorning the back. There was a wide grin on her face.

For so long, she hid her beauty beneath the anger she had been feeling over Adrian's death. She realized it was time to finally let go and move on with her life.

"Why, am I holding myself back from being happy and loving again? She thought. "Adrian and I had a wonderful life together and it angered me he had to leave me when we were just beginning to talk about having a family, a dream we both worked so hard to realize. And then, he's gone from my life forever."

As Felicia reflected, the elevator came to a rest and the doors opened to the lobby. She glanced around one more time and looked at her image in the mirror. For a moment she thought she saw Adrian smiling back at her as if to say it was okay for her to move on with her life.

As she refreshed her lipstick, she felt herself beaming once again. "*God and Adrian,*" she thought. "*Sent Michael to help her let go.*"

Jerry Bristol greeted Felicia in the lobby as usual. He tipped his cap to her as she exited into the cool night air.

Cal was on time as always. There was a degree of respect Cal and Felicia shared with one another, being on time. As she made her way to the silver Rover, she heard a hearty burst of laughter coming from inside the vehicle. Cal was seated in the passenger side ready to jump out and hold the door open for Felicia. His back was turned as he chatted with Michael. He never noticed her creeping up to the window.

Felicia pressed her freshly painted lips upon the clear glass and embedded her lips against the window. Cal jumped, surprised by Felicia's sudden playful behavior. Then he laughed and nodded to Michael and said as got out to open Felicia's door. "Don't know if it's the new account or you Michael but this is the Felicia I haven't seen in a long, long time."

Michael just sat there mesmerized by the perfectly planted outline of Felicia's lips on the window as the door swung open and she slid in next to him. As she looked over at Michael, she wondered what effect, her actions had on him and smiled.

"Okay, to the two men in my life, business is done, now it's time to head home, order some dinner, open a bottle of red zinfandel, put on some music, comfortable clothes and relax. Oh, Michael I did not forget you." Felicia put her hand on Michaels arm. "I will show you to your room so you can shower and get comfy as well while we wait for our scrumptious food to arrive."

"*This is great.*" Michael said to himself. He had travelled over three thousand miles to begin a life of lonely nights and sad songs and instead he was feeling an easiness about everything, including himself. He drifted back to the morning and the emotions he felt leaving his life behind. Then he remembered what Melanie had said.

"I am not certain what our future holds and will let it unfold the way it is supposed to."

"*Maybe.*" Michael thought. "*This is the first chapter in my new life.*"

Cal pulled out into the Frisco evening. Traffic had died down considerably since they first dropped off Felicia. The sun was getting ready to take its journey towards the night and stars started roaming the waterfronts skies. The gulls flew almost sedately.

The threesome made their way through all this serenity and headed on to the Golden Gate bridge. The clangor of metal reminded Michael of the first time he had driven over this magnificent structure. He glanced back into the city lights and raised his hand in a mock salute to a place he had come to know over twenty years ago.

Cal turned off at the exit just past the bridge. Pleasant Bluffs was a rustic but exclusive row of houses edged along the Sausalito Cliffs. Felicia and Adrian had purchased their dream home two years before he died.

The seagulls followed the trio along the narrow roadway.

Many of the houses along Pleasant Bluffs were built in the late forties. Alexander and Charles Gooderheim, were the key architects for many of the cliff side dwellings. Their trademark was the handmade stain glassed door that graced the front of these natural wooden homes.

As Cal turned into the driveway, Michael peered out the window at two, six feet high, tree like sculptures on each side of the gated entrance. Felicia looked over at Michael eyeing the sculptures. "They are totem poles carved by the Pacific Northwest's, First Nations people. Adrian had those made for me in British Columbia and shipped to adorn the entrance before we moved in. He was always doing something unusual when it came to gifts."

As they pulled past the gate, Michael thought about his own connection to where these carvings came from. He recalled the many days he would pack a lunch and hang out on the side of the Provincial museum in Victoria watching the native artists carve totem poles.

Things were too fresh in their relationship, but Michael knew eventually he and Felicia would have time to talk about the connection they shared with British Columbia. He remembered many a book he'd read about people coming into your life for a reason, a divine connection, fate or just being in the right place at the right time.

Michael had always believed in the divine connection aspect, just as, he had experienced the voice on the beach.

Cal took Felicia's bags as Michael swung the strap from his leather carry all over his shoulder. The thirty plus minute drive had taken them from the lighted city streets of San Francisco to a haven of beauty and solitude.

The night air was much cooler now. Michael took a deep breath and stepped towards the front entrance to the house. Felicia, Cal and Michael stood at the large wooded door witnessing the California sunset through the stained glass.

The door swung open and Felicia entered the sunlit alcove. Michael stepped aside to let Cal past him. He stood in the doorway almost breathless as the image that had so politely filtered through the entranceway glass was now a fiery, red disc emblazed across the back wall. It filtered itself magnificently through a large picture window.

"*Ahh.*" Michael thought to himself. "*The sunsets on the West coast were nothing short of spectacular.*"

Chapter 8

Moss Colored Carpet

Moss Colored Carpet

As Felicia walked towards the kitchen, she paused to spend a special moment with some heartfelt memories.

She looked across the shiny floors at the scattered sunlight. The evening colors were bouncing across the floor. She then looked out into the bay's sky and perched her head slightly higher so she could see the rippling waters below. She breathed in softly and closed her eyes. There was a sense of easiness filling her. As she whirled slowly to her left, she caught a glimpse of Michael's silhouette standing in the alcove.

Her heart began to remind her of all the wonderful feelings life can offer. She let out an easy sigh that felt so reassuring.

Felicia brought a smile to her lips once again as she thought to herself poetically. *"True love never really goes away, it is waiting to be reborn in another part of your soul."*

Michael seemed to hear Felicia's thoughts and turned to look at her. No words were exchanged, the visual exchange said it all.

Felicia turned and walked towards Michael, her hand outstretched. "Let me show you where you will be staying." She said, as she slipped her hand into his.

The evening was so calm.

Cal had changed and was heading to Stanford University to stay with friends for the weekend. Looking at the two of them as they headed to Michael's quarters and nodding in approval, he bid farewell saying, "Have a great time getting to know one another."

As Michael unpacked his things, Felicia headed to her room.

After living in designer clothing all week, she was content slipping on a pair of old jeans and a sleeveless shirt. To observe her, it was as if she was walking on air. Feeling euphoric and deeply relaxed she, made her way through the long corridor. Her hair cascaded off her shoulders across her smooth tanned skin.

She was like a chameleon.

Felicia Stouffer could blend in anywhere at any time. She was quite stylish. Her beauty had heads turning everywhere she went. Her peers not only admired that she created her own style but that she was strong and persevering.

Voices in the local circles spoke of her with great compliments. When Adrian was in the picture people who knew them would ask them to share their secrets for a successful relationship. There was an undying curiosity how the two could stay so in love and remain sane about one another with all their successes and the pressures of the corporate world. Adrian would simply say that he and Felicia believed that true love could conquer all.

Michael had unpacked, changed into sweats and a tee shirt and was standing in front of the bedroom window admiring the night skies. Felicia pulled up to the door of his room and peered in. The molding around the door felt cold as she pressed her cheek against it.

With wide eyes, she watched quietly as the moon's light bounced off Michael's squared shoulders. It was dark now and the moon's light was reflecting across the bay's waters.

Felicia began to feel a pleasing warmth inside as she stared into the room. Michael's hair glistened from the light.

"You know Felicia, this is exactly how I wanted to be able to see San Francisco this time. I knew there was a divine reason for coming here now." Michael said as he focused his thoughts across the moonlit waters below.

Felicia seemed to be subtly startled. She wondered how Michael could have known she was standing there.

Michael turned around from the window and faced Felicia. His physique resembled that of an athlete, not a poet. He seemed so attuned to his body as he walked towards her. Felicia entered the doorway. The two paused a few feet from one another. Michael reached into his pocket, placed a silver medallion in Felicia's hand. Looking into her eyes, he spoke. "Keep this close to your heart always and the true light of love will always be there to guide you."

Felicia looked down at shiny winged figure resting in her half-closed hand and smiled. "I think I will call him, Gulliver."

Michael replied. "Cute, sea-gull, Gulliver."

They walked side by side into the huge, open kitchen. Michael loved to cook. The sight of the hanging cookware caused his culinary desires to run wild. He always told Melanie that a true passion for cooking was the secret to the good life.

As he prepared dinner in their little kitchen on Park Street, Michael would raise the spoon or fork to her lips to sample his creation. Melanie would always part her lips slowly and laugh as he placed a taste of his latest recipe upon her tongue.

With its deep orange terra cotta counter top at the center of the room, the array of gourmet cookery suspended from the ceiling, Michael felt as if he were in a Parisian bistro. He had thoughts of donning an apron so he could begin preparing a gourmet meal for Felicia. Just then, the doorbell rang. Michael's train of thought was broken.

The food Felicia talked about ordering earlier had arrived from The Lotus Flower, a local gourmet Thai-Polynesian restaurant that Felicia considered to be the best in the Bay area. She had extensive dining experience, having sampled food from all over the world right here in America. Los Angeles, Seattle, New York and of course, San Francisco, every city had its own range of ethnic foods to experience. When Felicia recommended a place or a dish from a menu, you knew it would be a, five stars, culinary experience.

The table was already set and there was soft piano music playing in the background. Michael was the same way. His mother taught him to always be prepared with a set table, candles and background music so guests would feel invited when they came into the home.

A bottle of red zinfandel from the Shenandoah Valley graced the table. The wine sat breathing as Felicia put the Javanese Beef, a charcoal broiled marinated sirloin, Mai-Kai escargot, Red Dragon rolls, and Mahi-Mahi tacos onto serving dishes.

Felicia loved to unwind with music at the dinner table. Tonight, her choice was a blend of Celtic harp and violin.

As she and Michael sat, Michael poured the first tasting of the zinfandel for her. She took a sip, pursed her lips and gave a smile of approval. The choices Felicia made for this meal were out of this world. With each bite, Michael was in heaven.

He loved to prepare foods using a variety of spices and sauces and had created some remarkable dishes. Nothing he had conjured up in the past could compare to this. "I guess I have to expand my horizons if I am ever going to be able to satiate this lady's appetite." Michael's thoughts turned from cooking to Felicia.

As the two sat quietly gazing at one another throughout the scrumptious meal, a wave of mental images flashed through their minds. Felicia kept thinking about the romantic dinners she and Adrian had shared over the years. Michael thought about Melanie and him as they waltzed across the floor at breakfast. Each had their own past filled with loving memories. Even in thought, Felicia and Michael found themselves caught up in the good feeling of their first evening together.

It was now after midnight, less than a day after Michael said goodbye to Melanie. Although the clock was moving him away from the life he had known, the time engaged with Felicia seemed to stand still. *"How could this be?"* Michael thought to himself. "I know, I still love Melanie. Why am I feeling so far away from her right now?" He felt himself at such ease in the moment sitting there with Felicia. "Snap out of it!" He told himself.

Felicia was whirling with her own thoughts. Her situation was different then Michael's. She'd been alone for four years and was waiting for a moment like this to move on with her life. "How can I find myself feeling attracted to a man who just left his wife not to begin a new relationship but to begin a new life. Am I wrong or being selfish for feeling so comfortable with him? I mean I met him on the plane for God's sake less than a day ago."

As perplexed as they both were in their own minds, each questioning the righteousness of their feelings, there was no denying a special friendship was forming.

At one point, Felicia politely excused herself in, an effort to, pull herself away from the emotions that were drawing her more and more to Michael. She walked over to her collection of music and began filing though the records perhaps looking for something more upbeat. The soft music was beginning to conjure up erotic thoughts in her mind. She hadn't been with a man in a long time and did feel drawn to Michael not only from what they shared emotionally on the plane but physically from the first time she peered into his room, to the energies she was feeling from across the table.

As Michael's eyes followed Felicia's every step, he began to think of Melanie. Although he was feeling certain desires, he kept thinking of her, their memories and, the situation he was now in. He had called her as the plane touched down and told her of meeting Felicia and the invite, she had extended to him until he could get on his feet. At the time there was no reason for either one of them to think of the meeting as anything more than a friendly gesture.

For Michael or Felicia to feel that the unplanned meeting at nine-thirty the previous morning would aspire into something? Only a divine intervention knew that.

A piano's melancholy chords entered the dining area from the living room. There was no change in the tempo of music. Michael turned to focus his thoughts to Felicia as she entered the room.

The dining room was one of the most romantic rooms in the house. Often, Adrian and Felicia would spend hours sitting here talking into the early hours of the morning. There was an engaging way of conversing that took place between them. Both were attentive listeners. Both shared their honesty about anything that may be troubling them but in a loving way. They were well educated and could touch base on a vast plane of subjects.

Being spiritual and in tune with the higher forces of the universe through the years they practiced yoga and metaphysical studies, they seemed to rise above the everyday things that dismembered most marriages.

Their exchange of ideas, the ability to respect one another's opinions without judgement and the willingness to compromise when needed kept their relationship going strong. And, there was the unexpected little surprises, spur of the moment getaways and their love for the simple beauty in life.

They had an extensive music and movie collection and a floor to ceiling library. When they felt the need to unwind, they would often attend self-help seminars to expand their horizons as individuals and as a couple. Friends would gather in their home for an evening of bliss. Stocking feet was the norm while dining. One needed to feel the soft, moss colored rug under their feet. The thick carpeting gave a person a feeling of incredible calm as they sat at the table.

While most of the home has an open, airy feeling about it, the dining room wraps its décor around you and lets one feel as if they are in a tropical paradise. This was where the entertaining took place.

Felicia and Adrian loved sharing the secrets to the success of their marriage. An invitation to the Stouffer residence was an experience. From the food, to the view, to the couple that presented it, while it may have all seemed on a grand scale, Felicia and Adrian even with their wealth, were quite humble and down to earth. This was why they were admired and loved by so many. Felicia had lost this over four years ago and for the longest time, wondered how she could ever carry on without the love of her life.

Michael raised his glass. "Felicia, you have shown trust in me not only by inviting me into your home but by sharing so many personal aspects of your life. Often, we think anything good in life is just that, too good to be true." Michael went on. "Sadly, we often miss out on life's rewards because of our fears. If either one of us had been afraid to talk to one another when we got on that plane, we would have missed out on the beginning of our friendship."

Felicia reciprocated by raising her glass to Michael. "I have longed to trust again and have spent many nights wondering if I would ever find someone I could love, wholeheartedly." Michael rested his glass against Felicia's and thought. *"To trust and love wholeheartedly. Everything she and others said about them as a couple sounded so perfect."*

Life wasn't always filled with the excitement of being together. It all looked good on the outside but, there was also something about Adrian, Felicia never shared with anybody. Would she eventually be able to open herself up to Michael?

Chapter 9

Missing Piece of The Puzzle

Missing Piece of The Puzzle

The dawn's light was beginning to come into the morning as Michael and Felicia were still engaged in conversation. Felicia began to tell Michael about Cal.

"After Adrian's passing, I was shattered mentally. I was ready to call it quits, sell the house and move back to British Columbia. I told him I couldn't bring myself to driving anymore. That is when Cal came into the picture. The doorman in my building pulled me aside one day and told me about a young man he knew who would be perfect for the chauffeur's job. Caleb Connor was like a son to Jerry Bristol, much like Jason Congdon had been. Cal had taken a security job at The Bristol Building while attending Stanford. A hulk of a figure at six feet five inches tall and a solid two hundred and thirty pounds with a blonde crew cut and blue eyes. He was a promising NFL linebacker until he blew out his knee in his junior year.

As soon as he mentioned Cal, Felicia said without any hesitation, "He's got the job." She had known him from working the front desk. He was always respectful to her. When he heard of Adrian's death, he had flowers sent to her office.

Jerry Bristol arranged for Felicia and Cal to meet and the rest is history.

Felicia opened up to Michael about her relationship with Cal. "Cal has been more than my driver, he has been a friend and my strength during some hard times. He trusts my judgement, that is why he so readily accepted you. Cal has had his own tragedies in life losing his parents in a car accident when he was twelve. He was raised by an abusive uncle. A football scholarship to

Stanford was his ticket out. He was set on playing pro football until an injury ended his aspirations. So, you see Michael, he and I have this working relationship that lets us be the best of friends as well."

Felicia continued. "I have often wondered if Cal was the reason, I was never able to meet someone. I mean, Michael, do you think men were afraid to approach me because of him?" She said with a grin.

Michael let out a hearty laugh. "Perhaps guys see the size of him and are scared stiff to get near you! I would suggest getting someone smaller to drive you around." Michael said jokingly.

Felicia looked inquisitively at him and asked. "Did you feel intimidated by Cal when you first saw him?"

"I had no reason to be." Michael said. "I was already with you when I met him."

Felicia got up and moved to the other side of the table to sit next to Michael. She reached over and put her hand on his arm. He turned to look at her. "You're absolutely right." She said looking directly into his eyes. She wanted to feel her lips pressed against his at that moment but instead leaned closer, put her arm around his shoulder, and gave him a soft kiss on his cheek. "Thank you, for being you."

Michael pulled away slowly, put his hand on Felicia's shoulder and spoke. "I came here, not to run from Melanie but because I needed the time alone to find the missing piece of my life's puzzle which was to write a book. I was so afraid of being swept up in loneliness and guilt that I would forget the real reason I left and return a defeated man. You have shown me that I can have people in my life who respect and support my dreams without expecting anything in return except seeing me happy." He eased Felicia off her chair. They now stood face to face. "You are a rare find in life."

The huge star shaped clock on the dining room wall was now approaching six. The skies were beginning to turn a pale yellow as a light fog hovered over the bay.

Felicia and Michael had been up throughout the night engaged in storytelling. The same scenario had taken place between Felicia and Adrian long before Michael had come into her life. This night held a special meaning. The seeds of a long and lasting friendship had been planted.

It was time to rest, they gave each other a soft hug and retreated to their rooms at each end of the corridor.

As he lay there, Michael sent Melanie a subtle text message. "Settled in finally, long night just talking and sharing stories about our lives. Monday, I go into San Francisco to begin looking for work so I can get my feet on the ground. Felicia says I can stay until I find a place. Very fortunate to have found new friends like her and Cal. Going to get some sleep, miss you, love you, sweet dreams."

As she lay there, Felicia sent her own simple mental message. *"Adrian, I know you would have wanted me to be happy. I met someone who reminds me so much of you. Along with Cal, I now have a new friend in my life."*

Chapter 10

The Plymouth Rock Inn

The Plymouth Rock Inn

Sunday was a much, needed day of rest and relaxation for Felicia and Michael. They ate a late breakfast. Michael arose before her and strolled down to the kitchen where the coffee pot was ready to go. He turned it on. As the aroma filled the air, he poked his head in the fridge, found what he needed and surprised Felicia with an "atmosphere omelet."

Unlike a conventional omelet where the egg is folded over, this is a process whereby the eggs are covered while cooking so they rise and surround the ingredients. Once prepared and put onto the plate, it looks like a fluffy cloud. Michael made this one with fresh tomato, chopped up onions, a spritz of Worcestershire sauce, freshly chopped basil leaves and feta cheese.

Cal had gone grocery shopping the morning we arrived so there would be fresh food for Felicia while he was in San Jose. Little did he know there would be a welcomed guest preparing breakfast for her.

Felicia smelled the coffee brewing as she waltzed into the kitchen. The omelet was already at the table artistically garnished with fresh strawberries and pears. A glass of fresh orange juice and cup of coffee adorned each plate. As he pulled out her chair, Felicia was all smiles. "My gosh Michael, and you cook too!" With each bite, Felicia looked across the table pointed her fork at her friend. "mmm, mmm, absolutely heavenly. Wow, I have never eaten an omelet like this in my life!"

Even though she had a dishwasher, Felicia wanted to wash the dishes the old-fashioned way. She washed and Michael dried, and the table was reset.

"How about if we just lounge around since we both have a busy week and watch a movie?" "Great idea." Michael replied.

The living room had a large half-moon shaped sofa. As Felicia looked through the movies, Michael got comfortable, sinking deep into the soft cushions. As he sat there, he kept his eyes on Felicia. She wore white silk pajamas and a flowing robe tied at the waist. Michael was still in his sweats.

She settled on, "Under the Tuscan Sun", a romantic story about a newly divorced woman who goes on a tour in Tuscany and purchases a villa and starts a new life. Seeing what she had chosen, Michael said. "I have seen it three or four times and absolutely love it, great pick." As she walked back towards the sofa, the silken material flowed across her body like an angel's wings unfolding. Michael gazed at her strolling towards him and felt his heart skip a beat.

Halfway through the film, Felicia paused the screen and headed into the kitchen. Within ten minutes she had created a small tray filled with a loaf of fresh semolina bread, an assortment of hard cheeses, cut pieces of Italian salami and olives. She paired the delectable tray of food with a bottle of Pinot Grigio. It was a match made in heaven.

That night Michael and Felicia discussed their plans for the new week and headed to bed early. As he lay there, Michael thought about his book, not Melanie. Felicia assured him again during their conversation earlier that he had a place to stay until he was ready to move on. *"Funny how in just two days".* He thought to himself. *"This woman and I have become so comfortable together."*

There was still so much more the two of them would share.

Six o'clock was the time Felicia left for the office to avoid the traffic going into the city. Cal was already outside and waiting when she and Michael emerged from the house. The morning was atypical of the bay area. A heavy fog rolled in over the water from the cool night and blanketed the Golden Gates arches. As the trio made their way downtown, the fog had already begun to lift.

As they pulled up to her office, Jerry Bristol approached the car. As he opened the door to let Felicia out, he peered in to bid Cal a good morning and noticed Michael sitting next to her. Before he had a chance to ask, Felicia spoke up. "Jerry, I want you to meet Michael Langston. He is here from New Jersey and will be staying with me for a while. He may be dropping by the office from time to time so please tell the people at the front desk."

"I will, by all means, Mrs. Stouffer, by all means."

Michael reached over and took the Englishman's hand in his. "Nice to meet you, Jerry."

As she turned towards her office, she tucked her hand under Jerry's arm. "See you both around four-thirty, going to make it a short day." For her, ten hours was a short day. She would normally be at the office till 6:30 or 7:00. The two strode up the steps and disappeared through the shiny steel doors.

Now that Michael was staying with her, she was looking forward to her life after work and now felt, she had no reason to keep herself at the agency that many hours. She also knew there would be business trips when coming home would be out of the question but, she had an agency to run, clients to appease and now someone besides Cal to share her down time with.

Michael asked Cal if he could be dropped off at Fisherman's Wharf. He wanted to spend the day getting acclimated with area. *"I am sure so much has changed."* Michael wondered to himself as Cal pulled up to a small coffee shop across from the wharf. "Thanks for the ride, I will walk back to Felicia's office from here and see you at four-thirty."

"Sounds great." Cal responded. "Have a great day."

Michael stopped at a local newsstand and picked up the paper. He knew he would have to find a way to support himself until he could earn a living writing. He headed back to the coffee café, took a table outside and ordered a cappuccino. The morning sun was glancing off the waters. Michael turned his chair towards the bay took a sip of his drink and let the warm rays caress his face. He loved the sun as much as he loved the water and wondered why it had taken him so long to get back. He glanced out at the bay and smiled, turned his chair back to the table, picked up the newspaper and began looking at the classified ads.

Perhaps it was his state of mind at the time, but nothing seemed to spark his interest. He did see a few listings that he could consider but he knew he would be defeating his purpose for coming here. He knew his writing habits well. Once he got into his book, he knew he would be completely submerged in his writing.

What he needed to do was something new and different, something that would pay decent money yet not tie him down to a nine to five routine. He had committed himself to everyone else for too long and wasn't about to fall into that rut again. San Francisco was full of great eating places. He turned his attention to ads for waiters.

He had worked as a waiter before settling into the corporate scene and managed to make a good living. The hours would be in tune with his writing. A job as a writer wasn't easy to come by, a job as a waiter was. He circled three ads that looked interesting took another sip of his now cooled drink and gestured to the waitress. Michael pointed to his cup. As she approached with a new mug of cappuccino bubbling over with whipped cream, Michael folded the paper and placed it on the seat next to him.

A familiar voice interrupted his train of thought.

"Hey handsome, could you use some company?" Michael turned to see Felicia leaning over the railing. "*She looks absolutely, exquisite.*" He thought to himself as he accepted her invitation to join him. "What brings you down here so early, I thought I wouldn't be seeing you until four thirty?" Michael asked.

"Oh, I was in one of my moods. I come here when I get like that." Michael seemed concerned. 'Are you okay, is anything bothering you?"

"Nothing at all." Felicia replied. "I used to have a small office down the street. Ever since I moved up to the high life, this place has become my escape, the water relaxes me. It helps me keep my life in sync."

"What about you Michael?"

"The same." Michael replied. "I really cherish this environment."

Felicia ordered an iced cappuccino. Michael picked up the newspaper and showed her the ads he had circled. "Why a waiter when you are a writer?" Felicia asked. "Didn't every artist wait on tables before they became famous?" Michael joked. "I guess you're right, I did myself. When I had my studio down here things got tight financially so I took a job at night waitressing. If it wasn't for that job, the studio would've gone under." Felicia glanced at the ads, took another sip of her iced drink and motioned for the check. "I have a meeting at eleven, going to head back. I will see you and Cal at four thirty." Michael rose to pull Felicia's chair out for her. As she turned to leave, she gave him a kiss on the cheek.

Michael thought about calling Melanie, but he pushed the thought aside as he touched his cheek.

As he sat sipping his cappuccino, his phone rang. It was Felicia. "For some reason, I began thinking about the place Adrian and I had our first date. I remember him standing in the doorway of my shop. He wandered in asking for directions, said he had an interview and wanted to make sure he was headed in the right direction. His voice was so soothing."

"I walked him to the door and reassured him he was. He thanked me and headed up the street. That morning I began daydreaming about him. There was a soft demeanor about him. I could sense his gentle nature and air of confidence. His cologne was new to my senses but one I was mesmerized by. If peace and intrigue can describe a scent, that is the best way I could describe it. The smell was so pleasantly intoxicating. It lingered in my store and on my mind the rest of that day." Felicia continued her story.

"A few days later he came back in telling me he had gotten the job and wanted to thank me for helping him out by treating me to lunch. I motioned towards the dock and pointed out a little place I frequented for lunch. Then I thought, that might be a nice start for you. I think you will fit right in."

She said the place was a haven for aspiring artists. While pursuing their dreams, actors, musicians and writers would work at the Plymouth Rock Inn.

"Michael, I know the servers make pretty good money. Many of my friends and colleagues go there for lunch and I know they tip their servers very well."

Felicia said she knew the owner and was certain she could get him in for an interview. "You know, Felicia, that sounds like a great idea. I never thought I would be looking for a job as a waiter but like you said, it's a start."

"Maybe I can meet you at the inn around 3:30? I thought I would be here longer, but my staff has everything under control. We had a short meeting about the new account, and they all agreed to furlough me out of here early. They said since I had worked hard to get the Adams account, I deserved to go and celebrate." There was excitement in Felicia's voice. "We can have a drink and a bite to eat and celebrate your new job."

Michael laughed. "I haven't even had my interview yet."

"I know you'll get It." Felicia responded. "You belong there."

Within fifteen minutes after he and Felicia hung up the phone rang. "Hi, is this Michael Langston?"

"Speaking." Michael replied.

"Michael, my name is Dana Evans. I just spoke to Felicia and she said you might be interested in working for me here at The Plymouth Rock Inn. If you are available around one thirty this afternoon, I would love to meet with you."

Michael couldn't believe how quickly Felicia made things happen. He looked at the clock, it was now twelve forty. He folded up the newspaper, finished his coffee and headed over towards the Plymouth Rock Inn.

Michael arrived at the inn and walked inside. Several patrons were lounging around sipping coffee, working on their laptops or just engaging in intimate conversation.

The inn was warm and cozy. There were nautical artifacts draped from nets hanging from the rafters. Paintings of ships and seascapes adorned the walls. There were no tables just fluffy pillowed couches and chairs, kind of like the sofa in Felicia's living room. Coffee tables were situated in front of the seating to hold drinks and food. The place reminded him of a cafe in The Village in New York.

The staff greeted him with an exceptional warmth. Michael felt comfortable exchanging greetings with everyone that walked his way. Thinking about what Felicia had said about fitting right in, he smiled to himself. Most of the servers were pursuing an artistic endeavor. Their jobs here were an escape into a world where they could energize their spirits and have some fun.

Being an aspiring author, made Michael feel right at home.

"Hi, Michael, I'm Dana, we spoke on the phone a short time ago." He extended his hand to greet her. She motioned for him to join her on one of the couches. "Can I get you a cup of coffee or something to drink?"

"Coffee would be perfect, thank you." Michael replied.

"I understand you are a friend of Felicia's. She told me you were new in town, a writer and a great, great guy." Dana kept the other compliments Felicia shared about his looks as their little secret.

As she looked across at him, she was taken aback by his resemblance to Adrian.

Michael looked at the slender bodied blonde and smiled. 'Well, I guess Felicia filled you in on me already. I would love to do breakfast and lunch, this would free up my evenings for writing. Is that something that you can accommodate?"

"By all means Michael, how is eight in the morning until two in the afternoon?"

"That's perfect." Michael responded.

"Can you come in tomorrow morning to get familiarized with everything?" Dana asked next.

"That works out fine, didn't expect something to happen so quickly, thank you. I will see you tomorrow morning." He shook Danas' hand and headed out. It was only two o'clock, so he had some time to kill before meeting Felicia. He pulled out his phone to call her with the good news.

"That is so wonderful, I knew you would get it. So, what are you going to do until we meet?" As Michael glanced up and down the street, he noticed an old book store and a couple of thrift shops. "Going to go into some of the shops and hunt for treasures." He said, his voice filled with excitement.

"Now that sounds just like something I would do." Felicia answered. "See you at the inn at three thirty."

"See you then, Felicia, have a great day."

First stop was the book store. The little kid in him came out as he rummaged through the bins. As he searched, he drifted back to a troubled time in his life.

Chapter 11

A Mentor and A Teacher

A Mentor and A Teacher

Michael was relieved he had landed a job so quickly. He knew too much idle time on his hands was no good. He had seen how becoming disassociated from having a purpose would lead him down the wrong path. Because he had so much creative energy bottled up inside of him any distraction would cause him to lose focus on his dream of becoming a writer. His pen would silence, and he would fight inner demons trying to tug him in every direction but his true calling in life.

Michael was never one to understand or accept anything in life that held rigid boundaries. He was the who would step to a different beat of life's music. He was one whose existence on this planet would be one that would leave behind an eternal etching of beautiful poems describing nature and spiritualism that would be ingrained in hearts all over the world.

Michael Langston knew this from a very young age. Conformity held him back.

When he tried to settle and conform to rigid ways, his quest to pour out his creative juices were put on the back burner while he tried to appease other's expectations of him. Relinquishing his dreams, he would focus all his energies working long hours. As his inkwell of ideas dried up, he tried to justify his purpose with a paycheck. Michael would pull out his journal, pick up his pen and try desperately to get back on track, to no avail.

Perhaps it was the stagnant waters he was treading. Perhaps it was an underlying energy, a realization or a calling that made him throw in the towel.

Michael could feel Melanie's every emotion as she tried to paint a clear and precise picture of life, one that did not include being, "The Poetry Man."

When he came to the realization of what he was doing to himself, he handed in his resignation, left his life behind and boarded that flight to San Francisco.

Felicia seemed to sense what Michael needed in his life from the beginning. It took Melanie years of watching him struggle to finally let him go. Although she couldn't bear to tell him, Melanie had drawn the curtain on her life with Michael the moment the cab pulled away from Park Street.

Only two people in the writer's life ever really understood him, his grandmother and Marcy Holt. Now, it seems there was a third, Felicia.

Lillian Langston was Michaels maternal grandmother but most importantly, the one who mentored him from a very young age. After she passed away, he thought of how she had taken his hand and led him to his most prized discovery.

From the time he was old enough to walk, the library became a place of solace and escape into a wondrous world of words. His grandmother would sit him down and read aloud, great literary works. The flow of poetic ballads painted beautiful pictures of nature in Michael's mind.

As he got older, he penned poems much like he had envisioned from the words that were read to him as a child. The ocean's waves didn't just crest upon shores, they walked over the sands in liquid bare feet. The heavens became a canvas for God's airborne creatures to paint with their wingtips. A forest in the moonlight, opening to a whole new universe just by how the rays filtered through the tree's limbs. Michael created a vision that took him beyond the pages of his journal. He wanted to honor his grandmother for all she had done for him growing up. He envisioned a natural retreat of log cabins, a lodge and a lake, a place aspiring writers, musicians and artists would go to feed off, of one another's creative energies. The dream was so vivid in his mind. It would be known as, <u>Lillian Pines</u>.

When Michael was eighteen, he spent as many weekends as he could on one of the small Gulf Islands north of Victoria. He would take a twenty-five, minute ferry ride over from Nanaimo and hike about half a mile from the dock into the woods. There he would retreat to a one room log cabin with a couple of battery operated, lanterns, food and water, and his journal. This is where he would be at one with nature while he wrote. A simple life, yes, just the way he wanted it.

It was a world filled with a beauty all its own. The eagles would fly overhead as if they were protecting the island from that peace being disturbed. The waters would wash upon the shores with a gentle ease. The natural life was what surrounded you. The wild life was what came to visit you.

It was on this island Michael Langston envisioned Lillian Pines. He pictured log cabins scattered along the wooded inlet. Each artist would be able to enjoy complete privacy. The quiet, beautiful surroundings, soothing sounds of the calm island waterway. Nights filled with fresh air and star filled skies. *"Ah, how that would enhance any creative mind."* He thought to himself.

Michael painted a clear picture of Lillian Pines. *"There would be a main house or lodge which would boast high ceilings with logged beams and rafters. From the rafters suspended lanterns that could be dimmed at night while a stone fireplace filled a huge, open living room with warmth. There would also be an extensive library that would overlook the sitting area below. Here artists could gather and share stories and experiences."*

There were two other things that had to be at Lillian Pines. A lounge appropriately called, "The Poetry Café" and a small gift shop where he could sell works from other artists.

Much of the dream began to formulate right after Michael left high school, the words of another mentor encouraging him to never give up writing.

In high school, Michael would spend his days escaping the structured world of classroom learning by burying himself in his writing journal. Often, he would get caught putting his poetic expressions down and be asked to leave the class. This was a punishment he thrived on because it allowed him the chance to delve into his own world. There was only one teacher that knew what was going on inside of the young poet.

"Michael, whatever you do in life, don't ever give up writing." Marcy Holt was the person at school who clearly understood Michael's lack of academic motivation. She was the only one who knew how to channel his creative energies. Marcy took him under her wings and nourished his creativity. She would spend an hour each day after school letting him write out his feelings on paper.

Mrs. Holt loved teaching. Students in her English classes were encouraged to write. She would take a subject most students had no interest in and turn it into a world of individual self-expression. Michael Langston thrived on this and she knew it from reading his poems.

By the end of the year, she knew Michael would never be content unless he was doing something with his life that involved writing. As he continued glancing thorough the works of Shakespeare, Poe, Whitman and others, he pictured the moment he stood in the doorway of Marcy Holt's classroom listening to his mentor's words of encouragement. He remembered her small frame, how she exuded such an air of dignity when she read the works of William Shakespeare.

She would look out at the students as if she were upon a stage, leap forward with passion as each sonnet's words passed over her small, deeply rouged lips, She, would look out from her tightly pulled back jet black hair, eyes slightly affixed on me as she read.

"Remember Michael don't ever give up writing." Were words that never left my heart. As the memory of the inspiring teacher began to dim and he found himself glancing down at the bin of books once again, Michael's eyes fell upon a small red hardcover book with a title that captured the journey down memory lane he had just taken.

As he approached the register, he laid down the book and felt a sense of peace. The title read: **"The Sonnets of Shakespeare"**

Michael left "The Forever Engrained" Bookshop, his book tucked happily under his arm. He was quite amazed at his find. Ironically, it was a publication from 1976, the exact year of the copy Michael's grandmother had given him to cherish. That copy lay on a bookshelf in the little apartment on Park Street signed: "To My Grandson, May, these words inspire your own as you become a writer in your own right."

As he strolled along the wharf, Michael stopped to peak into several of the little shops. What was lovely about these stores was that they were all family owned from generations ago. They were keeping up the traditions their forefathers had built their dreams on. The facades with their old-world charm, as one pecred into the windows, was like taking a trip back in time, a time when fishermen would anchor their boats along the wharf at the end of a day at sea and venture in to tell tall tale stories and celebrate getting back to shore safely.

The sign read: "If you love her, she will love it." As Michael peered in one window front, something sparkling caught his eye. He went inside and approached the counter. A woman was behind the counter organizing the shelves. She saw Michael approach through the glass case and rose up to greet him. "Well, good afternoon young man. And what would my pleasure for you today be?" Her English accent brought a smile to his face but more remarkably was the woman's resemblance to his grandmother. She had the same high cheekbones, silver hair, green eyes, and wore the same style of half rimmed glasses. As she peered out over her glasses Michael looked over her shoulder and pointed at the small earrings hanging in the window.

"What a lovely choice." She said as she handed them to him. She explained that they were made from jade mined in British Columbia, Canada. As he held them in his hand, Michael recalled buying his grandmother a necklace made from the same stone. "I am very familiar with this jade having lived in BC, that is what attracted me to them. I know someone very special who will love them as well."

Before he exited the shop, Michael looked at the clock behind the counter. It was now a few minutes before three. He would be meeting Felicia soon at The Plymouth Rock Inn where they would celebrate his new job. He had just enough time to mail out a package.

It had been a few days since he and Melanie had any contact with one another. Michael called her and left several messages including Felicia's address.

He called and left another message. "Hi, it's me. Haven't heard from you, hope you are okay. I landed a job today, not quite corporate but it's a start and will give me time to begin concentrating on my dream of writing a book. Sending you a surprise, let me know you received it."

Michael entered a package mailing store, placed the earrings in a small box and mailed them off to Park Street. The clerk assured him, they would arrive in two days and gave him a confirmation number to track the package.

Chapter 12

Inspiration

Inspiration

As he made his way back towards the Plymouth Rock Inn, the gulls were flying overhead. Michael looked up and began to recall the last time he was in San Francisco. He remembered the trip he had taken past Alcatraz Island. Before boarding the boat, he had gotten a sandwich and a bag of chips. The gulls followed the boat from harbors side. Michael would soon be sharing his lunch with the spirited flock. The silver medallion he had given to Felicia the night they arrived, represented his winged friends.

Michael read a story years ago about a seagull named Jonathan. It was the message in that story that let him keep his dream of someday being able to make a living from writing. Of all the things he could do in life, writing he felt, would enable him to be his own person. Free from corporate America was where Michael longed to be. That story about a persistent gull planted a seed about his purpose in this world.

At the tender age of thirteen, Michael penned a poem entitled, "Wind Swept Sea." The dream of The Poetry Man began to take flight with that writing.

After learning how to do calligraphy in art class, the aspiring poet found an artistic niche for presenting his writings. He would take his best poems and do them in calligraphy on yellow parchment paper, frame and sign them. He had delivered five of these to a gift shop in Victoria to be sold on commission. The shop owner was quite impressed at young Michael's entrepreneurial spirit. The five original poems he brought in had a price tag of fifteen dollars. Because he believed he had to clearly envision his dream in order to make it come true, he felt there was no better way for him than to sign his works, "The Poetry Man."

Felicia had returned to the office after meeting with Michael, a new-found energy exuded from her. The family at 21st Century Advertising office noticed a sudden perk in their boss and began to wonder if there was someone new in her life.

Her assistant knew her better than anyone in the building except Jerry Bristol.

Jackie began to compare the Felicia of now to the one that had stood so strong since her first day on the job. She couldn't help but to conjure up thoughts about her boss' vibrant aurora. She knew deep inside that some kind, of love had reached into Felicia's heart since she came back from New York.

As the office chatter began to concentrate on Felicia's sudden change, her assistant kept her thoughts to herself. She knew it would have to be some very special kind of man to sweep her off her feet. Jackie knew Adrian, she had seen the two of them blossom throughout the seasons and watched as Felicia did her best to stand tall as much as she was hurting inside after his death.

Jackie Rodriguez had been Felicia's executive assistant for over ten years, she knew the sparkle in her boss, was more than the new account she had just landed.

Michael arrived at the inn at three twenty. He was always ten to fifteen minutes early, that was his nature.

He took a seat on one of the fluffy couches and ordered a water with lemon. He would wait to order the wine when Felicia arrived so they could share a celebratory toast together.

Melanie looked at her phone as she had done for the past few days. She knew the messages were from Michael. It had been less than a week since he left and while she tried so hard to miss him, her emotions just weren't there. *"It's sad"*. She thought to herself. *"How two people come to a place in life that no matter how much they think they love one another, there are other intangibles pulling that love apart."*

Melanie had grown up in a family where marriage was forever no matter what. There was no room for exploring dreams that did not include the other. The family stayed together and worked any issues out. Many a time it was not about love but about a commitment to the vows. "Through thick or thin, in sickness and in health, till death do us part." This was how Melanie saw her parents being able to remain together all those years. And like Michael, she tried so hard to hang in there. Times and values had changed for them and coming to a point of realization that their marriage was not working as tough as it was to accept, became inevitable.

Melanie looked at her phone once again. She listened to the messages but could not respond. She knew eventually she would have to.

Michael looked at his phone. Still no response from Melanie.

As he put his phone back in his pocket, the door to the inn opened. The sun at her back, Felicia walked in. Dana ran up to greet her. They gave one another a big hug, exchanged a few words Dana then walked Felicia over to where Michael was seated. "Your usual Felicia?" She asked. "Not tonight, this is a special celebration." Felicia glanced over at Michael. "Since this is your night, I am in with whatever you choose." Michael looked up at Dana.

"You've known this woman for quite some time, I think I will let you surprise us and make the wine and food choices."

Felicia smiled. "I like how you handled that one, Michael."

"Well, I am just curious to see what I will be serving you for lunch when I wait on you." Felicia gave him a soft tap on the arm. "I promise, I will be an easy customer when it comes to ordering."

"By the way, I called Cal and told him to pick us up here around six." Felicia looked at Michael and winked. "I know you have your first day at work tomorrow and don't want to keep you out too late."

"Cute." He responded.

Dana personally waited on her longtime friend and new employee. She joined them in a toast to celebrate Michael's arrival, new job and Felicia landing the new account. As she hosted her glass to them, Dana spoke from her heart. "To my dear friend Felicia, may this be the beginning of a new chapter in your life, one filled with much deserved happiness, health and love." And, to you Michael. "Welcome to your new start in life, you have a wonderful friend in Felicia, a great place to work and may all your literary aspirations unfold as you too begin a new journey." With that the glasses were raised and a cheer of, "salute" rang out.

As they savored their dinner, Michael noticed Felicia was wearing the medallion he had given her. Felicia caught him looking and remarked. "I love it and will treasure it always."

They finished up dinner around five thirty and headed out to wait for Cal.

Felicia tucked her arm under Michael's as she had done at the airport. Together they walked along the dockside, stopping a few feet from the inn to gaze out into the bay. There she was in all her splendor, the Golden Gate Bridge.

Michael pulled his phone from his pocket. No word from Melanie. He turned to Felicia and began to speak. "I found a pair of beautiful jade earrings and mailed them off for Melanie this afternoon. I am not sure why, but she hasn't answered any of my messages since I arrived."

Felicia untucked her arm, took Michaels hand in hers and looked at him with compassion in her eyes. "The hardest thing is accepting loss in one's life. I am sure Melanie is feeling her own pain right now and just needs time alone to work it out for herself. As long, as she hears your voice, she knows you are okay and that is all you can do at this point. Michael, just keep her assured as you are, by letting her hear you are okay. Trust me, whatever it is, she will eventually reach out to you."

"Hope I didn't interrupt Ms. Stouffer." The couple turned around to see Cal standing next to the Rover with the back door open. On the way home Felicia sat with her hand over Michael's arm. He was looking out the window as they crossed the bridge reflecting on the words shared with him about accepting loss. If anyone had to deal with loss in their life, it was Felicia and here she was giving him reassurance that everything was going to be okay.

Michael showered and met Felicia in the kitchen. He'd prepared a cup of tea for the two of them. "Well, tomorrow is my first day and to be honest, I am a bit nervous." Felicia tilted her head back looked right at him with those emerald eyes and laughed. "You, Michael Langston, the aspiring author, nervous? You have one of the sweetest personalities and that is not just coming from me, Dana said how you just make people feel comfortable around you. Just be you and the rest will be a piece of cake."

After tea was done, Michael excused himself from the table. This time he strode over to Felicia and gave her a hug and soft kiss on the cheek. "Thank you for your friendship and for everything you did for me today with my new job and your comforting words."

"Michael, you sold yourself, I just made a phone call."

Cal had already said goodnight and retreated to his loft above the garage. He stayed there during the week and unless Felicia would be returning home from a business trip, he would leave right after dropping her at home on Friday evening and spend weekends with one of the many friends he had. No matter where he went, He was always back in time to take Felicia to the office bright and early Monday morning.

As he lay in bed, Michael's thoughts turned to his first day at work and giving thanks for all the good happening in his life. Then he thought about the earrings he'd sent to Melanie.

Chapter 13

The First Kiss

The First Kiss

Morning arrived soon enough. Michael put on his jeans and a white button-down cotton shirt and his top siders This was the dress for The Plymouth Rock Inn. As he was exiting his room, Felicia was coming down the hallway towards him. They met and shared a morning hug and hello and as had become the thing with them. One or the other would give a kiss on the cheek.

Felicia slowly pulled back from their embrace and looked Michael up and down. "Wow, you look handsome, love the shirt."

Michael always loved the look of a woman who wore a white cotton blouse tucked into her skirt or jeans with heels. Felicia had on the white cotton blouse, a silk emerald green skirt to match her eyes and a very light pale shade of lipstick and, her "Gulliver" necklace.

As they were hugging, Michael was drawn to the faint scent Felicia had on. He remembered it from years ago. It was an erotic scent of middle eastern spices. "I can't quite remember the name, but I do remember the scent and it has been years, did not know anyone still wore it. It is the most beautiful scent, to be honest, I was about twenty-one when I first experienced it. I was with some of my buddies playing pool in this small bar. Out of nowhere this scent hit me. It actually made my knees weak." He said with a laugh.

Felicia looked at Michael feeling a warm flush running through her after his story. "It actually is a perfume I have been wearing ever since I was in high school and no one has ever really complimented me quite the way you just did. And by the way, I did notice your cologne, an earthy, spice blend, sandalwood?"

Michael was mesmerized. Felicia had hit the nail on the head about the scent he had on. *"What a way to start off this new life."* He thought. *"Here, I have this woman whom I just met but feel like I have known her for years."* Although out of politeness, Michael never asked Felicia her age, but he did know that she was older than him based on some of the timelines she shared. She mentioned leaving British Columbia to attend college in Washington five years before he graduated high school. In his mind, Felicia was five or six years older than him.

She was a very attractive woman who was well rounded, strong and intelligent. He saw her intellect in the conversations they shared, her choice of music, movies and tastes in art, wine and food. The fact that she was the head of her own company had Michael questioning at times how she with so much going for her, would feel so comfortable being with a man who was starting all over. She was already established, her course already charted, he was a man who was setting his course to a dream of writing his first novel.

Michael pondered on it for a moment. "I would love to know the answer to that one day. For now, I think I will just enjoy this wonderful journey. The rest is all irrelevant."

Michael began to wonder if those feelings of self-doubt, when things were going well, that they were too good to be true were setting in then, he thought about the hug he had just shared with Felicia and shrugged all his potential worries off.

The job at the inn was moving along wonderfully. Michael was able to adapt quickly. His customers loved him and remarked to Dana how attentive and personable he was. His genuine smile and knack for storytelling as well as being a good listener had repeat customers requesting to be seated in his area.

Felicia came in a few times a week to have lunch. As much as Michael asked her not to leave a tip, she would always take care of him. He would put the tips she had given him aside and surprise her with a gift to thank her for all she had done for him.

The money was better than expected and Michael knew when the time came for him to get his own place, this job would provide more than enough revenue for him to meet his expenses.

Three months after he arrived, one of Cal's friends received a job offer on the East Coast and her apartment would be available. As much as he was enjoying his time with Felicia, he had promised her as soon as the time came, he would get his own place.

Cal took Michael to see the apartment. It was on the fifth floor of an old warehouse that had been converted to lofts. The place was wide open and spacious, over fifteen hundred square feet with windows all around. The ceilings were ten feet high with studio lighting throughout. Cal's friend was a photographer. She said all the furnishings would be left since she would be moving to New York and starting out fresh.

Candice Bergdorf had known Cal in college, and they had remained friends ever since. He would visit her on weekends from time to time and they would go on photo shoots together. Cal was an avid photographer himself.

Candy freelanced for a wine and culinary magazine based out of San Francisco. She loved travelling throughout the Western states doing her craft. California, Oregon and Washington offered some of the most picturesque landscapes and estates. She recently began venturing further North into Canada's wine region which offered interior waterways and rugged cliffs. The backdrop against the vineyards made for even more incredible photos.

The Okanagan Valley, in British Columbia, had been producing wines since the middle of the eighteenth century. It boasts a climate that is warmer and more arid than Napa Valley. The region gets nearly two hours more sunlight per day during the peak growing season which helped to create a distinctive taste in the wines.

After travelling to the valley and tasting these delightful red and white varieties, Candy was curious as to why Okanagan Valley wines had not been a part of her magazines buy list. While the region was known for its winemaking she discovered, the wines don't travel far from where they were produced unless brought out of the region by visitors from outside of the province.

Her trips across the Canadian border gave Candice Bergdorf a whole new perspective on freelance photography. She was an avid traveler but most of her trips outside her magazine's assignments were self-funded. She sent a letter to Conde' Nast with a proposal to do wine country tour photo layouts.

Her desire was to be able to see the world and get paid for it. In her cover letter in which she included her resume and samples of her work, she proposed accompanying tour companies throughout the world's wine producing countries as a photographer for the company's travel magazine.

Within three weeks, Candice was invited to meet with her perspective new employer. The offer was made prior to her going to New York which she readily accepted. It was just a matter of shoring up some minor details, securing a place to live and setting up the date for her arrival at her new job. The opportunity Candy had created for herself opened yet another door in Michael's new life.

Michael reached out several more times to Melanie but heard nothing. Because he was so caught up in working and settling into his new life, he never noticed the card from the post office. Felicia had placed the card on the kitchen counter. Almost two weeks passed, and the card still sat where she left it.

At lunch one afternoon as Michael placed her avocado salad on the table, Felicia looked up him and said. "Michael, I see the card to pick up a package from FedEx is still on the windowsill in the kitchen. I am sorry but I guess I forgot to tell you and we have both been so busy that it just sat there." Michael responded. "I actually did see it but thought it belonged to you."

That night Michael looked at the card. It read: *"Undeliverable, Return to Sender, please pick up at the Market Street drop off center."* Michael knew exactly what was in that package yet had a hard time understanding why Melanie hadn't returned his calls. *"At least,"* He thought to himself. *"She could've called and let me know what was going on inside her head."*

Felicia walked into the kitchen and saw the card in his hand.

Michael excused himself and headed up to his room without the customary evening routine he and Felicia had of sharing a cup of tea and conversation about the day's events.

As he lay there looking at the card, there was a knock on his door. Felicia opened the door slightly, poked her head in and asked. "Do you want to talk about it?" Michael propped his pillow up against the headboard and motioned for her to come in. She walked over and sat down next to him. "You seem to have something on your mind, it's not like you to just walk away like that. I know something is bothering you and I am a little concerned, that's all." Michael showed her the card from FedEx.

"I sent Melanie a gift a while ago which I guess based on this card, she never accepted. All the times I called and left messages without a response, then this." Felicia took Michael's hand in hers. "I know I told you a few weeks ago that she would reach out to you when she was ready. I can't really explain how Melanie handles her pain. I do know I shut down after Adrian's death. Michael, when you left to come to California, losing you could've have been like the death of your marriage to her. I am sure she is grieving, and I am also sure, she will reach out to you however that feels comfortable to her when she feels ready."

Michael knew things were going pretty good for him. He had a job he loved making good money, had just landed an incredible apartment and of course Felicia as a friend. At that moment Felicia leaned over. "Could you use a hug?"

As Michael pulled himself towards her, those jade green eyes looked right into his.

For the first time, neither one turned to kiss the other on the cheek. Their lips met and they shared their first real kiss. It was soft and subtle. They both pulled back, looked one another in the eyes and smiled.

Chapter 14

Return to Sender

Return to Sender

Candice called and left a message to tell Michael it would be okay for him to stay at her place which would soon be his, while she spent the weekend in New York City setting up her new apartment. Conde' Nast had included a two, bedroom condo as part of their job offer. She said he could come by after work Friday since she would be taking a late flight out that night.

He called her on Wednesday to work out the details.

"Hi, Candy, it's Michael. I got your message and spoke to Felicia about it. She told me at lunch today, she will be going up to Vancouver this weekend to visit her parents. She thought it was a great idea."

Candy replied. "My place is within walking distance from the inn, you can come by after work, I can give you the keys and show you where everything is. I also have something interesting to talk to you about." Michael accepted the invitation and said he would see her Friday.

He had gone by the FedEx Store, showed the card and his ID and picked up the returned package Monday after work.

The first kiss he'd shared with Felicia on Sunday, stayed with him but he knew it was something that just happened in the moment. When he opened the box and saw the earrings, his thoughts were interrupted by thoughts of Melanie and he began to question her behavior. *"What the hell is going on with her. Does she sense something. Is she thinking Felicia and I are more than friends?"*

Thursday evening at dinner he poured his heart out to Felicia about the questions racing through his mind. "I can accept everything you presented to me in, regards to Melanie's feelings but I am kind of stuck between a rock and a hard place right now between what is going on with her and how our first kiss affected me." He looked at her and went on. "To be honest, I don't know how you felt after our first kiss Sunday night because it happened under some very emotional circumstances but, it felt wonderful to me."

Felicia, took a sip of her wine, put her hands under her chin and focused on every word coming out of Michael's mouth. "We had that kiss and then you went off to your room. There really was nothing to it right?" He went on.

"That night as I laid in bed, I had this feeling, like a teenager who had kissed someone for the very first time. The words to a song kept running through my head. I really couldn't shake it out of my thoughts. The song was called, "Starting Over" by John Lennon.

"For some reason that single touch of our lips had me thinking about how parallel our lives really are. How we met. How It was like we had known each other for years, existed in different parts of the world and were destined to come together in the exact moment we did."

Tears began to fall from her beautiful eyes as Michael went on. "I kept thinking about you losing Adrian and me leaving Melanie but until I picked up the package, I never felt I had lost her. I remember thinking the first weekend we were together how fortunate I was that even though we were miles apart, Melanie was still in my life. My whole perspective on my relationship with you changed on Monday as I walked out the door with that package in my hand.

Michael leaned across the table, took his napkin and wiped the tears from Felicia's cheeks.

Felicia took both his hands folded them in hers and began to speak. "Michael, I believe in the power of God's healing and I believe he has healed my pain by bringing you into my life when He did. That kiss was more than our lips touching Michael. In that moment it washed over me because it was so pure and innocent, but it has stayed with me as a reminder that I can and will feel the wonderful feeling of love again." Michael was now affixed on Felicia's every word.

"This may sound selfish on my part, but you know what Michael, if Melanie were to tell you it is over between the two of you, I would be right there to pick you up and take you into my arms. What you and I have does not replace anything that was in our lives before we met and as you said, it is like starting over. As crazy as it may sound to you right now, I would gladly begin a new life with you if that is God's intention for us."

Michael could feel his own tears gathering at the corners of his eyes.

"Michael, as much as I felt drawn to make our first kiss last and last, I couldn't out of respect for your situation."

"Yes." Michael said shaking his head in agreement. "We both could've given in, I am sure it would have been beautiful but, in our hearts, we both knew it was not right to give in to our emotions. As a result, we've kept our relationship where it is supposed to be for now. I agree with you wholeheartedly, only God knows what tomorrow has in store for us."

The day at The Plymouth Rock Inn with filled with anticipation. Michael was curious about the comment Candy made to him about wanting to talk about something he might be interested in. He made sure it didn't distract him from his customers, but he couldn't help feeling anxious. She had already offered him her place fully furnished. What else did she have on her mind.

As he was preparing for the lunch crowd, he heard a familiar voice call out to him.

"Hey sweet friend, brought along a special guest." Felicia was walking towards him with none other than Candice. He sat them down in Felicia's favorite spot by the window.

"Now, this is a pleasant surprise". Michael looked over at Candy. "I didn't expect to see you until later this afternoon." Candice smiled back at him. "I was going to wait until you came over to share something but after speaking to Felicia, I decided it couldn't wait."

She pulled out a small portfolio from her laptop case laid it on the table and opened it up to the recent photo shoot she had done in the Okanagan Valley wine region and pointed to one of the pictures. "Cal and Felicia told me about your aspirations of writing a book. I understand from what I have heard, you have quite the talent for writing. My gift is photography, not writing. I began thinking after what my friend here shared that maybe you might be interested in doing some freelance writing."

Michael was taken aback by Candice's proposal and began to grin from ear to ear. "Wow, never in a million years would I have guessed this is what you wanted to talk to me about. I did try doing freelance for magazines years back but, I got sidelined by the rejections. I took them to heart never realizing it takes a lot of perseverance and faith to keep at it until that letter of acceptance comes your way. This was why I set my dream aside. Then I had this recalling, a voice from the past telling me it was time to focus on my dream." He pulled his shoulders back and looked at the two women with an air of confidence. "Coming here was my commitment to never giving up on my dream again. All that has fallen into place since this beautiful lady sat next to me on that flight and reassured me, I was going to turn my dream into a reality."

Michael reached out, took Felicia's hand in his and looked over to Candy. "With all she has gone through, she never stopped believing in herself. She has instilled such confidence in me. And now you come into my life and without even knowing me, offer me this opportunity to write not just words based on a subject but words describing the things that mean the most to me, the beauty of nature."

He got down on one knee in front of them. "How thankful and blessed I am to have both of you in my life. I really don't know who I should propose to, you both have swept me off my feet." The two women looked at one another and smiled.

"Well, Michael." Felicia squeezed his hand. "I saw you first so if there is any kind of nuptials going to take place, it will be with me."

They all shared a hearty laugh.

"Well, ladies, I do have to get to work, it's lunchtime and this aspiring author has to earn his way until he creates that number one bestseller."

Chapter 15

Freelancing

Freelancing

The weekend at his soon to be dwelling was quite the experience. Michael hadn't been alone for quite some time. The hardest part for him was to not get too caught up in thinking about the past but instead to utilize the time with positive thoughts about the future and all it held. Candice had given him the portfolio of photos and suggested he pick out his favorite six and try doing a magazine article that would, compliment them as well as tell a story. Storytelling was Michael's forte. He knew he would have to research some subject matter, that was something he'd always loved as well.

Once he sat down to write, Michael became engrossed in the process. Having this time alone proved to be very productive both in terms of using the time well spent and preparing himself for his new future, living by himself.

By Sunday afternoon, Michael had finished up a rough draft of an article he entitled, "The Vines Intertwined."

Taking from the photographs Candy provided, he interlaced the history of wine making in the region with a story of a couple experiencing it for the first time and deciding this is where they would exchange their vows. It was probably a different approach to photojournalism but nonetheless, Michael liked how it all "intertwined." Candice of course, would have the final say.

As he lay on the couch looking out the big studio window, the sun was making its way across the city. At eight-thirty, Michael's phone rang, it was from an area code he was unfamiliar with. He decided to answer the call.

"Hi Michael, its Felicia, I wasn't sure if you'd pick up or not but thought what the heck, give it a try. I was thinking about you this weekend and wanted to hear your voice and see how things were going. Candy told me she was giving you your first writing assignment." Felicia paused then went on. "I hope I didn't disturb you."

"Absolutely not." Michael replied. "I was just lying here by the window watching the sun pass over, what a great place." He then asked. Felicia, have you ever been here?" Felicia responded. "Yes actually, I have many times. Cal introduced Candy and I two years ago and we have had some memorable moments at her place. Some weekends when I didn't want to be in my house alone, I stayed with her. I just needed some company and she was there for me. We had some fun times, sharing stories, trying out the different wines she brought back from her trips and just having a girl's night out. Don't know how I will do that once she goes to New York. I guess we will have to visit one another."

"Sounds like the two of you really have a great friendship." Michael said. "The ironic thing about all of this Felicia is how everyone I have come in contact with through you interconnect somehow, and now I feel I have become part of that circle."

"Oh, but you have. Everyone loves you. What isn't there to love about a guy who writes poetry, can cook and is just a, great person. And." Felicia sounded excited. "My mom and dad don't even know you but can't wait to meet you."

"You told them about me?" Michael asked. "Didn't have to Michael it was written all over my face. As soon as my parents saw me at the airport, they knew there was something going on in my life. So, while you were chilling out at your new place." Felicia said almost as if to be sarcastic. "I was being interrogated about this new man in my life." Felicia laughed. "The reason I came up to Vancouver this weekend was to tell my parents about you and how we met and how happy I have been. I showed my mom a picture I took of you at the Plymouth Rock Inn in your white shirt and jeans. You know what she said Michael?" Felicia's voice took on an almost sexy purr. "mmm, mmm, very hot my dear daughter but I didn't think you were into younger men."

"Oh Mom." Felicia said she gave her mother a love-tap on the shoulder and explained. "We are only five years apart. Yes, I guess you could say I am the older women in his life, but it really isn't like that. We are good friends. He respects me, I respect him, and we enjoy one another's company."

Felicia turned to another subject. "By the way, did you get a chance to do anything on that article for Candy?"

"As a matter of fact, I did pour myself into it and just finished the first draft before you called. I gave it a different spin, more like a story than travel writing. Hopefully Candy will like the approach I took." Felicia's voice was filled with excitement. "That is so incredible that you wrote an article so quickly Michael, care to tell me about it?"

"I titled it, "<u>The Vines Intertwined</u>." It combines the history of the region and moves into the beauty of the landscape as seen through the eyes of a couple who are touring the region and they decide this is where they want their wedding to take place."

"Just like you Michael, the romantic." Felicia laughed. "I am sure Candice is going to love it."

Michael responded back. "How about if I copy it and email it to you. I would love to hear your critique."

"I would love that Michael, I can read it on the plane ride home and share my thoughts with you tomorrow night at dinner."

Michael sent her the article and made plans with her before their conversation ended for a five o'clock dinner in Chinatown. He asked her if she liked Peking Duck. "I love it." she replied. "Good, I thought you would, so I called them Saturday to place the order and make reservations for us."

Michael made a cup of Chai tea and curled up on the sofa. He lit some candles and put on, "Land of Forever."

As the serene sounds filled the room, he glanced around, took in a deep breath and smiled. He was feeling a sense of calm he hadn't felt in a long time. With the last notes of "The Calling" beginning to fade and, the sun having already set, Michael blew out the candles. Before he drifted off to sleep on the couch, he peered up through the big studio window and caught a lone, twinkling star and thought to himself. *"Someone up there is smiling down upon me."*

Chapter 16

Moving On

Moving On

Time was moving on for Felicia and Michael as well. It had been more than a year since they met on the flight from New Jersey. Through the departures of Cal and Candice to New York and Jerry Bristol to England and Felicia turning most of the reigns of 21st Century over to Jackie, the friendship between she and Michael took on more togetherness.

Michael knew it was time to move on and talk to Melanie. He called Felicia first. "Hi sweetie." Felicia loved him calling her pet names. "I really have to talk with Melanie when I get home. I just want to put closure on this so I can move on. I am fighting with my emotions and to be honest, it is really getting tough for me to hold back my feelings from you any longer." Michael stopped for a moment to give Felicia a chance to say something. She was quiet.

"I hope I didn't push it with you by telling you how I am feeling. Our friendship means the world to me, but I just want us to be able to take it to the next level if that is where we are destined to be." He paused and took a deep breath. "Felicia, I am watching everyone else evolve in life and relationships and really feel you and I need to do the same."

Felicia began to speak.

"Michael, it has been hell for me holding back my true feelings for you. Every time we are together, I just want to be totally submissive and not hold back. I do love that we have been able to build such a strong friendship, but I am ready for more with us, Michael. I mourned Adrian's passing for a long time then you came into my life and made me see I have a whole life ahead of me. We will be going to see Cal and Candice exchange their vows next

Spring. Jerry is retiring and starting a new life of romance with his childhood sweetheart. Even Jackie has told me now that she is where she wants to be in her career, she wants to settle down. It's our turn now Michael. I have loved you as my best friend now, I want to love you completely."

Michael heard every word Felicia said and knew what he had to do. He told Felicia he would call her after he broke the news to Melanie.

After his shower, Michael picked up the phone to call Melanie. Before he could dial the number, the doorbell rang. Michael looked through the peephole. An officer was standing at the door.

Michael edged open the door, the chain latch still secured. The man asked if he was Michael Langston. Michael told him he was. The man said he was from the Sheriff's Department and showed his credentials through the crack in the door to validate who he was. He then gave Michael a large brown envelope and said, 'You have been served." The address on the label read: **Melanie Langston, 34 Park Street, Upper Montclair, New Jersey**.

As Michael placed the envelope on the table next to the other pieces of mail he had picked up from his postal box, the tea kettle began whistling. While waiting for his tea to brew, Michael began feeling a little apprehensive about the correspondence from the Sheriff's Department and turned his attention to the other pile of mail. Sorting through, he saw the usual monthly bills and junk mail. There was one letter that stood out. Michael picked it up and glanced at the return label.

Ironically, a letter from Melanie had arrived the same day he was served papers.

Michael stared at the plain legal sized envelope as he sipped his tea, exchanging glances from the letter to the brown manila envelope deciding, which to open first. He picked up the white envelope and slid a letter opener through the fold and across. He pried the letter open, pulled out the folded piece of lined paper, unfolded it and placed it flat, next to his cup of tea and began to read.

Dear Michael,

The hardest thing I ever had to do was to wait this long to respond to you. I did get your messages, but I just emotionally could not bring myself to call you back. When you left that morning, I just wanted to let you go. When I looked out the window and saw you looking back, the tears just started falling and I had to rush to your arms one last time. Michael, when I told you I knew it was time for you to go, I knew in my heart it was time to let go of you. That was the hurtful part for me, knowing the dreams I thought we would build together had all but dissipated. When you left your job and told me of the voices calling you to write a book, I had a hard time relating to that. As much as I wanted to believe you would get to San Francisco and come to your senses about the life we had built together over ten years. In my heart as painful as it felt, I knew you would never be back once you left.

Michael, you are who you are with your dreams as I am with mine. I will never carry any hatred or anger over our not being able to live the American dream of having kids and owning a home. Simple, yes, that was all I ever wanted.

Remember, when you and I were going through some tough times and we went to marriage counseling? The counselor asked us to look at one another and describe the person we felt the other would be happiest with. Michael, you were very to the point and simple and you hit the nail on the head when you said. "She needs to be with a guy who wears a tool belt, a handyman type." Well, I connected with an old friend after you left who was there to offer support and friendship. You knew Rob Branco from coming into my parent's restaurant, he has his own plumbing business. He and I came to the realization that we shared the same goals and wanted to spend the rest of our lives together.

I trust you have found someone as I described on that day, a woman who never had children, was older and a professional business type. Michael paused after that line, took another sip of tea, looked over at a picture Candice had taken of Felicia for her "Business Woman of The Year" article, looked back at the last line he just read in Melanie's letter and smiled.

He continued reading.

Michael, when the papers arrive, all you, need to do, is sign and overnight them back to me. I have taken care of the rest.

I wish you, much health and happiness always,

Melanie

Michael folded up the letter, put it back in the envelope and reached over for the brown envelope. Pen in hand, he read through the contents. There was nothing to be distributed or children involved. As Melanie had stated, all that had to be done to finalize the divorce between them was to sign the documents and overnight them to her. He signed, took a deep breath and sighed in relief that there was finally closure. *"Well,"* Michael thought to himself. *"Everyone else had transcended into their new life, now it looks like Felicia and I can get on with ours."*

Chapter 18

The Earrings and The Crystal Angel

The Earrings and the Crystal Angel

Michael looked over to the star clock Felicia had given him as a house warming gift. It was an exact replica of the one she had on her living room wall. The time was now 11:23. He picked up his phone to call Melanie to tell her he had received the papers, signed them and would get them out to her tomorrow on his way to work. He quickly put it down. *"Why, do I need to call her, it is over."*

He picked up the phone again and dialed Felicia's number. She picked up on the first ring.

"Hello, Michael, I am so happy you called. I have been up, anxiously awaiting to hear from you. How did it go with Melanie?" Felicia asked.

"Well, much to my surprise, she beat me to the punch. After I got out of the shower my doorbell rang. It was an officer from the Sheriff's Department serving me with my divorce papers."

"Oh my God, Michael, really? Did you call her and ask her what was going on?"

"No, no reason to." Michael responded

Felicia let Michael talk.

"The other thing was, she had written me a letter which arrived in today's mail. I read that first thinking there was something in there to explain what the officer had handed me. Sure enough," He went on. "Melanie had never returned my calls because she knew from the moment I left, our marriage was probably over. The day I left, she thought I might have a change of heart, turn around and come back. I guess when I told her I found a place to stay, she knew it was the beginning of the end. That was why she never responded back to me and never accepted the gift I sent her. She cited our differences and felt that after ten years, it was time to let go."

"And how did you take all of this, Michael?" Felicia asked.

"As a relief, in fact, I just signed the divorce papers, sealed them back in the envelope and will get them out to her tomorrow. I say relief because there is no anger, the process is seamless, and she is already moving on with someone else." Michael stated.

"So, what happens now Michael?" Felicia's heart was racing. She was hoping he was feeling the same closure she felt when she was able to let go of Adrian.

"Honey." Michael said. "What happens now is that you and I begin enjoying our relationship in a whole new way. There is nothing holding us back anymore. We are both free to love one another now, to have the companionship we have been longing for."

"Michael, do you know, I love hearing you call me, honey. You have called me some loving names that close friends share but this time hearing that felt so different." Felica was beginning to get a warm-all-over feeling as she lay there listening to the man that she could now give herself completely to.

"Felicia, we have both waited very patiently for this moment. All the times I felt the urge to take you in my arms and just let myself go with you, I didn't, and you respected that. You never pushed me or gave me an ultimatum. And, that is how we were able to grow such a strong bond. I can honestly say, being celibate has really opened my eyes to the way I believe, God intended a man and woman to fall in love."

Michael explained his findings. "Over the years I read articles about couples and the things that either broke up their relationship or strengthened it. The keys I learned to success in long term marriages was that each person had first and foremost, respect for one another, an open line of communication, the ability to compromise, the acceptance of the other's individuality and most importantly, all of these couples viewed their partner as their best friend."

"My dear lady, I believe you and I have followed the most important key to building a long, lasting partnership." Michael paused.

"And what is that sweet, man?" Felicia asked.

"You are my best friend." Michael stated.

The clock now read 12:49. In four hours Michael would be getting up to head over to the inn. He wasn't feeling tired at all, if anything, he felt energized.

"Felicia, you must be tired." He asked knowing she had to be up early as well to go to the agency. "To be honest dear, I am wide awake and feeling wonderful."

"I had a fabulous idea and wanted to run it by you." Michael began to share his thoughts. "How would like to spend the weekend together at your house, totally locked away from the outside world. We could chill like old times, watch some movies, cook gourmet meals and share some fine wines?"

"It's funny you asked that my dear, the same thought was running through my head. I think it will be a great way to start our new life as boyfriend and girlfriend." Felicia laughed. 'How did you like the sound of that Michael, *"boyfriend and girlfriend?"*

'Sounds so cute sweetie, just like being in high school." Michael laughed as well. "I might even ask you to go steady."

"It's a date then." Felicia said. "I can meet you at the inn at two thirty, Friday after you get off. We can stop at that little market in Sausalito on the way to the house and get what we need for our meals. It will be fun shopping with you to see what we can conjure up."

Felica was enjoying driving herself to and from the office. She and Cal talked before he left, and she assured him she would be fine. Whenever Felicia and Michael went on their weekend jaunts, it was Michael doing all the driving.

Friday came quickly. The weather was perfect. The sun was shining brightly, the clouds were shaped like marshmallows, just floating slowly across the deep blue skies.

Everyone at the inn was more upbeat than usual. Dana was making her rounds with the lunch crowd, looking radiant as ever in a white chiffon blouse and jeans. Love was, in the air.

As Michael was waiting on his regular customers, he noticed a new, but familiar face. He walked over to the chaise she was seated in. "And, what would my pleasure for you today be ma'am?" The woman looked up from her bifocals and smiled when her eyes met Michaels. "I remember you, young man, you bought those lovely jade teardrop earrings from my shop, didn't you?"

"That English accent." Michael now knew exactly where he had run into her.

"Yes, I did buy those earrings from you." Michael reached his hand out to the woman. "It is so good to see you again. My name is Michael, Michael Langston." She put her other hand over his, took off her glasses, looked directly into his eyes and smiled. "Catherine Cheshire, a pleasure to see you again as well. It is a small world, I guess there is a reason for every meeting, for us it was when you bought the earrings and now at the Plymouth Rock Inn." Michael thought about what she said, then about the day he walked into her little shop. Catherine, with her English accent and looks reminded him so much of his grandmother. "How true." He said to her. "How true."

"So, tell me Michael, didn't that special person love the earrings?"

Before he had a chance to answer, Felicia was standing next to him. She looked down at the woman Michael was talking to. "Catherine." Felicia bent down and gave her a hug. Michael looked over at Felicia and said. "You two know one another?" "From the day I had my studio down here." She replied.

Felicia rose up from hugging Catherine turned and gave Michael a loving embrace. She pulled her head back then pressed her lips against his and gave him a soft kiss.

All the time Catherine kept her eyes affixed on them as if she wanted to say something but kept her thoughts to herself and just smiled.

When Felicia moved into her studio, she would frequent the little thrift shop looking for anything she felt would appeal to her visual senses. Art work, pottery, furnishings and even jewelry were treasures she had purchased from Catherine. When she moved into the Bristol Building, all those possessions came with her and now adorned her spacious office.

She and Adrian were friends with Catherine. He often stopped by the shop just to talk to her about his grandmother and listen to stories about life in England.

Upon hearing of Adrian's death, Catherine presented Felicia with a beautiful crystal angel and told her. "I wore this since I was a child now, I must pass it on to you." She hugged Felicia to comfort her and whispered in her ear. "Let this angel be your guardian and light when you feel despair and loneliness. You will find a new connection one day that will bring a rebirth to all the things you cherish including your love for antiquing and thrifting."

As Felicia reached down and took the angel now paired on her chain with the seagull Michael had given her, she realized how right this woman had been about her life. She put her arms around Michael's neck and looked into his soft green eyes.

This man opened her heart again and reignited her love for treasure hunting.

Chapter 19

Pampering

Pampering

Felicia and Michael strode out of the Plymouth Rock Inn for the first time in their relationship holding hands. As they exited, Dana was at the door to walk them outside. She turned to Felicia and said. "My dear friend, I have watched this blossoming and I am so happy the two of you can begin a whole new life together."

That morning, Michael had gone into Dana's office to tell her what had transpired. He was always able to talk to her and though she had just turned thirty, she had established herself as a savvy business owner just like Felicia; strong and independent and filled with an intuition about life well beyond her years. Dana had spent many hours over the course of the year talking to Michael about knowing when the time would be right to take the next step in his relationship with Felicia. She also knew Felicia had built strong feelings for him and couldn't wait for the day when they could be free to love wholly.

As she hugged Felicia, she pulled Michael in and put her arm around him. As the three stood in the doorway of the inn, Dana looked at the two of them and said. "I love both of you dearly and have prayed for this moment when the two of you would walk out of here as more than friends, maybe one day, it will be as husband and wife."

She held up a bag with a bow on it and said. "I have been saving these two bottles of wine ever since you started working for me Michael. When Felicia told me about you, I knew a time would come when I would be in this doorway saying, celebrate tonight like it is the first day of the rest of your lives." She gave Michael a kiss on the cheek and said. "Thank you for coming into her life."

The afternoon sun was beaming down upon the city. The day was still as beautiful as it had started. The clouds had given way to the heavens.

Michael pulled open the door of the Rover just like Cal had done so many times before. He took Felicia's hand and led her towards her seat. As she positioned herself, Michael tugged at the seatbelt and draped it across her body snapping it into its holder.

As Michael got behind the wheel, Felicia pulled down the passenger side mirror, brushed her hair and pulled it back across her shoulders. She took out her little makeup bag, put on eyeshadow, applied a fresh coat of her favorite lip gloss and dabbed a splash of Cinnabar on her neck and wrists. All the while, Michael kept thinking to himself how grateful he was to have her in his life. As Felicia was applying her cosmetics, she smiled to herself knowing the man sitting next to her loved everything she was doing.

Michael turned to her, leaned over, gave her a kiss and said. "Honey, I need to stop at my place before we head out to Sausalito. Just need to pick up something then we will be on our way to our first real romantic weekend as boyfriend and girlfriend."

Felicia said. "I am so ready my love."

He was in and out in ten minutes and deposited a small carry all bag into the back seat.

In no time they were on their way over the Golden Gate Bridge, listening to the same clanging sounds underneath the wheels Michael had experienced so many times before. First stop, The Sausalito Marketplace.

The other shoppers took notice, smiled and exchanged hellos as the couple wandered up and down the gourmet market's aisles side by side, each holding on to the cart. Felicia didn't look a day over thirty, not bad for a woman twenty-seven years older. And Michael, at fifty-two still had thick, wavy locks, a well-toned body and the same youthful looks as his lady.

Dana had remarked to Felicia in the ladies' room at the inn earlier that day, what a beautiful couple they made. "When I first saw the two of you together, I thought, wow, a match made in heaven." Dana said.

"A match made from heaven, Dana. Funny, I always felt Adrian did bring Michael and I together."

As they began gathering items and putting them into the basket, Felicia looked at Michael and remarked. "Now remember Michael, we will not reveal our secret recipes until we start preparing our special meals, okay?"

"It's a deal hon." He responded. "No disclosures until we have our first toast of Dana's wine."

Michael had decided on a simple dish consisting of raw oysters as an appetizer and steamed clams garnished with fresh parsley and hearts of palm in a mango sauce. Felicia's recipe consisted of fresh greens, cut up veggies, fruits and sunflower seeds with a raspberry champagne dressing and slivers of Reggiano cheese.

As Michael placed a bottle of Dom Perigone into the cart, he put his arms around Felicia's waist and said. "Tonight, we are going to ring in our new life together."

As they made their way past the gated entranceway and parked, Michael reached over and took Felicia's hand in his. Felicia turned to him and he put his hand across her shoulders and pulled her towards him. She tilted her head slightly. As their lips met, Felicia closed her eyes. The kiss was unlike the soft, respectful ones they had shared before as friends, this one was filled with passion.

All the times they felt lust or want for one another but had to restrain themselves with polite exchanges of feelings, now there was no reason to refrain from feeling total pleasure. As Michael pulled back, their lips sticking slightly as they separated, Felicia laid her head back against the headrest, looked at Michael and said. "You just melted me with your lips." He looked back at her, his heart still racing. "You did more than melt me, your kiss sent shivers throughout my whole body."

"By the way." Michael was grinning from ear to ear. "Don't think I didn't notice your amazing hair, nails and makeover. When you came to the inn, I wanted to ravage you right there on the couch but held back out of respect for Catherine."

As Felicia unlocked the door, she said to Michael. "I did a little shopping on my own this week and brought some special things to wear for you this weekend.

Felicia reflected upon her little shopping excursion. It had been a long time since she had any desire to feel sexy. A beautiful woman who always turned heads wherever she went, this was different, it was about feeling a sense of arousal as she tried on different lingerie. As she looked at herself in the mirror there was an underlying emotion running through the image being projected back to her. "Mmm," she thought to herself as she glanced up and down at her image, turned sideways then did a rear view. "I have been blessed with some good genes."

Felicia did take care of herself physically, spiritually and now that Michael was in her life, her emotional wellbeing was in check. There were no more nights of restlessness. She had done a complete one eighty and it showed as she studied every inch of her body in that mirror.

As she approached the checkout counter her eyes fell upon a section simply entitled, "**Romance**." She glanced over the various massage oils and scented candles. "*Why not,*" she thought. She placed several candles and two small bottles of oil in her basket. She left the lingerie shop and headed over to a little cosmetics boutique to get her makeup. A matured woman approached Felicia and offered to do a complimentary makeover. It was Friday, the beginning of the weekend. There were no deadlines, so Felicia checked out of the office right after her morning staff meeting and headed over to the wharf. She had spoken to Michael and told him she was going shopping for a few things before they met. He suggested she spend the day pampering herself. And, she did just that.

"Hi, hon, my name is Monica." She extended her well-manicured hand to greet Felicia. The woman looked incredible. Felicia guessed she had to be close to her in age. Her skin was flawless, not a wrinkle anywhere. She worked out to keep her body in desirable shape. If anyone was going to do a perfect makeover, Monica, would be the one for Felicia.

As she sat in front of the mirror, Monica began talking to her as she applied a lemon astringent. "First we need to get those pores opened, cleaned and toned." The tingly feeling told Felicia her pores were doing what they needed to do. The second phase was a soft clay rub mixed with eucalyptus oil for a deep clean. The scent from the oil as Monica exfoliated her face seeped into Felicia's sinuses. She closed her eyes and took slow breaths.

As the clay dried, her skin began to feel tight and firm. Next, Monica washed off the clay with a warm solution of rose water. Felicia was feeling like a spoiled woman. Little did she know, Michael was an expert when it came to facials.

While in college, each student in his Public Speaking class was asked to come up with an informercial lasting fifteen minutes. Michael had gone back to school at the age of forty to finish up his degree in Communications. From the time he was eighteen, he was giving himself facials.

He learned the art of skincare from watching his grandmother apply cleanser and cream on her face each evening. Her skin at ninety looked like a woman in her forties. Michael came to accept that it's okay for a man to take care of his skin. So began the era of facial applications not only on himself but the women in his life. They loved that a man could be masculine and appreciate the femininity of a woman.

Michael handed out the facial kit to each student and went through the process step by step. He joked with them as several guys looked at one another like he was weird. "You may have the face of an eighteen-year old now but if you want that same face in thirty years, this is how you do it." They knew Michael was much older than them. Many of them looked up to him as a mentor.

He wrote a self-help column in the college paper to answer the younger student's questions about relationships and, life in general under the pseudonym of, "**Dr. Insight.**"

Michael walked up to one young man sitting next to his girlfriend and winked at her. He looked at the young man and stated. "Jimmy, just think how much this young lady next to you would appreciate you doing something this special for her on date night." The professor and class laughed then, stood and applauded Michael for his creative and informative presentation.

Felicia had chosen the same color scheme for her face as Monica, all earth tones. "So, who is the lucky man?" Monica inquired.

Felicia reached into her bag and pulled out her phone and turned it so Monica could see her screen saver picture. "He is a very handsome man with a very glamorous woman." Monica remarked.

Felicia seemed to blush. "I feel like a twenty-year-old again. This man and I are in our fifties. It feels like time stood still wherever we were in our lives back then, catapulted us past what we have both gone through in getting to where we are today and then took us back in time to meet and fall in love."

"That is a very profound statement and I never would've thought you and I are around the same age." Monica revealed that she was fifty-nine.

Felicia believed in her heart that her and Michael's lives had crossed somewhere before.

Funny, Michael had the same gut feeling when he saw the totem poles from British Columbia gracing the entranceway to Felicia's house the first night he arrived.

Now, on to get her hair and nails done. Monica had complimented her a bottle of nail polish for her manicure at Changes Salon.

Jessie had been Felicia's hairdresser ever since she came to San Francisco. The aspiring stylist had just come to the bay area from Chicago to set up a new shop. She found a small storefront nestled in between the bookstore and Catherine's antique place, less than a block from Felicia's studio. She and Felicia met in the antique store. Both were buying things for their respective businesses and started chatting. Jessie needed Felicia to do some promotional ad work to get her new salon off the ground so, they came to a barter agreement. Felicia does the ad work, Jessie takes care of the hair and nails.

Jessie, was there to greet her as she walked in. "So, what are we doing today, sweetie?" Felicia responded. "I brought a picture to show you a style that caught my eye. I like the way it comes down across my cheek on one side and goes just past my ear on the other and is brushed back. Then, I would like to do something different as far as coloring. I thought a silvery-white mix of highlights, what do you think?" Felicia gave Jessie the picture. She looked at it and said. "I think it will look so sexy and alluring on you."

"Sexy, yes, alluring, yes." Felicia said as she envisioned the results in the mirror. "Let's get going on it then hon." Monica responded.

Felicia was all smiles as she eased back in her chair.

Chapter 20

You Make Me Feel Brand New

You Make Me Feel Brand New

Once they finished laying all the food out for their meals on the counter, Felicia went over to pick out the music for the start of their evening. Michael opened one of the bottles of wine Dana had given them. Bryan Adams, "Feels Like the First Time" filled the air. As she returned to the kitchen, Michael handed her a glass of the wine Dana had gifted them. Felicia raised her glass to him. "The lady who did my facial asked me who the special guy was. I actually wrote down what I said because it was as she said, so profound."

"I told her that I felt like a twenty-year-old again. That this man and I are in our fifties and it feels like time stood still wherever we were in our lives back then, catapulted us through what we have both gone through in getting to where we are today and then took us back in time to meet and fall in love."

"Michael, that is exactly how I feel when I am with you." Tears were falling as she touched her glass to Michael's. The tears were for the happiness she felt. There would be no more nights alone, even when she and Michael were in their own worlds. Felicia knew that when Michael started writing his novel, he would retreat into himself to allow the creative juices to flow. He had explained this to her over the course of their friendship.

As she looked at him, Michael remembered the time in his life not too long ago, he felt uninspired. "Felicia, the morning I got on that plane and I never shared this with anybody, I looked out the window and saw eyes looking back at me. At first, I thought they were Melanie's but now I have come to realize they were your eyes looking through me, touching my soul. The first time I saw your emerald greens, they became a part of me. Tonight, my toast to you is this." Michael reached his hand up and wiped a tear from Felica's cheek and put it upon his lips. "You have given me a rebirth of the things I cherished and believed in as a child and like a child, I got lost along my way. Now, I have you and every journey from here on in will never find me lost again."

He took Felicia in his arms and kissed her, this time, she pushed herself up against him. As they kissed, they danced their way into the kitchen.

"Well, my love, let's get started on our heavenly meal." Michael and Felicia stood side by side admiring their choices of ingredients. Michael put a deep sauce pan on the stove, diced up cloves of fresh garlic as the butter melted. Next, he chopped up the parsley leaves and added fresh clam juice for flavor to the pan with the garlic. Felicia watched in awe.

"Michael, have you always had such a passion for cooking?"

"Always, it is how I unwind and get my creative juices flowing." Felicia laughed. "You get more than my creative juices flowing just watching you, Mr. Chef Boy-O-Boy." Michael looked over at her and blew her a kiss.

As Michael was preparing his meal, Felicia set the table highlighting it with the fresh bouquet of flowers and tapered candles. After she finished, she peered into the kitchen. "I will be down in a few minutes sweetie, just want to slip into something comfy for dinner." Then she asked him. "Did you want to change as well?"

"You go ahead hon, I need to make my sauce and get the clams going." Michael replied.

"Is there anything you need me to do for you in here?" Felicia asked.

"Got it all under control but thanks for asking, see you in a bit." Michael answered.

Felicia headed upstairs while Michael got out the ingredients for the sauce. After cleaning and shucking the oysters, he put them on a bed of ice and garnished the dish with lemon wedges and the mango sauce. He placed the shelled clams in the pan to simmer in the garlic broth and chopped parsley. The aroma of the fresh parsley was appeasing to the senses. As she entered the kitchen Felicia complimented Michael on how wonderful everything smelled.

Contrary to what Michael thought, the term comfy for his lady was a white silk blouse with matching panties underneath. She had touched up her makeup, tied her hair back, put on his favorite spicy scent and left the top three buttons on her blouse undone to reveal the outside curvature of her perfectly shaped breasts. Michael took one look at her and mimicked a fainting spell, closing his eyes and falling softly to the floor. Felicia ran over and kneeled on top of him taking his arms and holding them behind his head. "Oh, my poor baby, let me give you a kiss to arouse you from this spell."

Michael just lay there letting Felicia do her thing. She kissed his face all over then began kissing his neck. As he began to squirm, Felicia raised herself upright, took Michael's hands and placed them around her waist. Michael was fully revived at this point and exclaimed jokingly. "Okay, first you make me faint with your outfit, now you are making my heart jump out of my chest kissing me all over like." Felicia squeezed her hands around his and gave him a sultry look. "It all worked, I brought you back to life."

You did that from the moment I saw you on that plane my love." Michael said as he sat upright and nuzzled her neck. Felicia let out a soft moan, tilted her head back and pulled Michael into her chest and whispered in his ear. "Now, you know one of my weak spots, later you can explore the other ones."

"Your turn to get into something comfortable hon, I will start on my special dish while you change. When you come down, dinner will be ready to go." Michael did an about face and made like he was staggering as he walked out.

"Damn, a hot kisser." He murmured in a low baritone voice.

"I heard that, Michael and you're not bad yourself." Felicia replied.

Going up the landing, Felicia had sprinkled rose petals on the steps. As he entered his old room, he noticed a note on the bed.

To My Beloved Boyfriend,

No need for you to sleep in here anymore, tonight, I want you in bed with me. Have been looking forward to the night you and I would be able to fall asleep and wake up in one another's arms. Amazing how we were able to abstain for so long.

Please come into "our" bedroom, I have a surprise waiting for you.

Loving You,

Your Beloved Girlfriend

xoxo

As Michael entered the hallway, there was a flickering emanating from Felicia's bedroom. The door was slightly ajar. He poked his head in. The California king sized bed was adorned with big, fluffy pillows and a thick down comforter. On the bed was a box with a bow and card next to it. Michael walked over, sat on the bed and sank into it. He opened the card first. It was a handmade card with Felicia's signature on the bottom.

Michael,

We planted the seed of friendship through the respect we showed one another. Now we can watch our love blossom.

Enjoy your gift...xoxo

He held the card in his hand and ran his fingers across the lettering. The card had the same black raised, embossed letters as the business card Felicia had given him on the plane.

He placed the card on the bed, picked up the box, slid the bow off, opened it and removed the tissue paper. Inside, there was a pair of black nylon stretch athletic pants and a black stretch muscle shirt and a pair of sandals. Michael took a quick shower, put his new outfit on and dabbed some Sandalwood cologne on himself.

As he made his way into the kitchen, Felicia looked up from the cutting board. She dropped the knife onto the counter and proceeded to play the same fainting act Michael had done to her. As she lay there Michael played copycat, got on top of her, pulled her arms behind her head and began kissing her face and neck. Felicia started squirming and tossing her head left and right. "Michael, you hit it again. My neck is very sensitive, I get aroused so easily with you kissing me like that. Keep it up and dinner may have to wait."

Michael got up and reached down to help her up off the floor. Felicia gave him a hug and went back to what she was doing. Michael brought the plate of oysters out to the table.

Anything special you'd like to hear with dinner?" Michael asked.

""How about that CD you brought me when you got the job at the inn."

"You mean The Neil Young one with the song, After The Gold Rush?"

'That's the one sweetie, it's right the on the top shelf."

When Felicia finished dicing the veggies and slicing the fruit, she laid everything out on a large platter over a bed of romaine lettuce. She sprinkled the Reggiano cheese, sunflower seeds and dressing on top and placed two cups of fresh lump crabmeat at each end of the platter. She adorned the crabmeat dishes with a garlic stuffed queen olive. Michael took one look at her preparation and knew he had found the perfect mate. All the things he tirelessly and lovingly did to not only cook a meal but to present it, Felicia showed the same passion in her culinary offerings as well.

The table settings with the recipes they had prepared looked elegant. After he situated her in her chair, Michael brought out the bottle of wine and refreshed their glasses. Instead of sitting across from one another like they would normally do, Michael sat at the head of the table and Felicia sat next to him. They were a couple now and desired to be close.

Felicia raised her glass and began to speak. Michael reciprocated pressing his glass against hers. "I look at all that is in front of me, a meal that would satisfy anyone, then I look at you Michael and you know what? If this table were bare and all I had was you I would feel completely fulfilled."

Michael reached over took her hand in his brought it up to his lips and said. "I adore being with you in any setting."

Michael picked up an oyster, dipped it in the sauces and placed it on Felicia's tongue. She rolled her head back and eased it down her throat. "These oysters with the mango sauce are out of this world, where did you ever come up with this recipe?"

"Actually honey, I just researched how to make the sauce and if it would mesh with the raw oysters."

"You definitely have the makings of a world-renowned chef. Did you ever think of going into the restaurant business?" Felicia asked.

"With you, anything is possible, book first though." He nodded at her.

Michael couldn't get over the salad arrangement with the crabmeat. Felicia crooned over the clams. Their feast was coming to an end. Neither one felt desert was necessary. They were pretty health conscious and did not crave anything real rich and gooey though they both had a fondness for cappuccino flavored ice cream. The fresh cut melon and strawberries was all they needed to top of the meal.

Felicia was not one to use the dishwasher. She and Michael enjoyed standing at the sink together, one would wash, the other dry. Tonight, was different Felicia had, another surprise in store and couldn't wait to show Michael. "Let's forego the dishes tonight dear, other plans." She refilled Michael's wine glass and told him she had some finishing touches to do upstairs before they retreated. As she put down the bottle of wine, she reached into the refrigerator took out the Dom Perignon and two flutes, gave Michael a kiss and waltzed up the steps humming to herself.

As he sipped his wine, he couldn't help but go over the picture he had in his head of how sensuous Felicia looked in her partially opened blouse as they dined. He played out a scene in his mind of him getting up from his chair, walking around and standing up behind her. He would bend over, kiss her neck and run his hands down her blouse across her partially exposed cleavage and around her firm breasts. Just then Michael's phone rang startling him from his thoughts. "Who the heck could that be?"

"Hello, my handsome man, you can head on upstairs now. I am all ready and waiting for you." Felicia said seductively.

Michael never had any reason to set foot in Felicia's bathroom as he had his own full bath in the room he stayed in while he was with her. Before he strolled down the hall to meet her, he stopped in his old room and pulled out a small box from the carryall he had packed for this romantic weekend. Michael had done a little shopping himself Thursday after work.

As he once again approached her bedroom, the door was now opened all the way, the flickering light was dancing behind the stain glassed door leading into the bathroom. The door was a custom request she had done by the builder. It was similar, to the one leading into the house with the same design as the entranceway, the sun over the bay with clouds hung under blue skies and flock of seagulls traversing just above the rippling waters. The rest of the room was dark except for the hazy light reflecting outward from behind the door. On the bed a small box sat silhouetted by the dim light.

Felicia saw Michael's shadow and called out. "That is another surprise for you. Don't open it just yet, it's for later. Okay, sweetheart, you can come in now."

Michael eased the door open. The bathroom was as palatial as the other rooms in the house. He looked past the dual marble sinks where his eyes fell upon Felicia. She was submerged halfway in the bubbly water, the top side of her perfect breasts resting atop the suds. The jetted tub was swirling the bubbles around her bronzed skin. Michael began to feel himself getting aroused and felt a little embarrassed. There was no towel anywhere in proximity to him, so he folded his hands over himself.

Felicia saw Michael's hint of embarrassment and said reassuringly. "Honey, it's okay, we can be fully open with one another now. It's a turn on for me to see you like that. Come on over and get in with me, you'll feel better awash in the bubbling jets."

Felicia stood up the soap running down her naked body and held her arms out. "Join me my love."

Easing his way into the steaming water, he snugged in next to his woman and put his arm around her. Felicia reached over and handed Michael a flute of champagne. "To you, my vivacious, intelligent and romantic lady." Michael said as he toasted Felicia.

The champagne was creating a relaxed state in each of them.

Felicia had poured some of the coconut oil she got in the lingerie shop into the tub. With the oil lathering their skin, Michael placed his hand on Felicia's thigh and began massaging it into her. She ran her hands across Michael's back and chest. As he slid his fingertips slowly up and down her leg Felicia pushed her lower body forward. She took his hand and placed it on her breast and began moving it in a circular motion. The erotic sensation they were feeling from all of this was like the art of Kama Sutra. Slow and gentle touches, just enough to arose without climaxing.

Felicia and Michael had talked about eastern eroticism and how different this lovemaking was compared to what they had learned about the birds and the bees. Practicing this method of physical contact was something they had agreed would be a part of their love life. Felicia had once remarked to Michael her feelings about applying what they studied into their relationship. "There are many couples out there who thrive on the rough and tumble methodology of sex. My study of eastern customs and my own personal preferences for engaging in romantic interludes can be defined simply by the words, slow and steady."

As the jets subsided, Michael cradled his arm around Felicia's waist and spoke. "I couldn't agree with you more. I believe foreplay is not something designed to take one over the edge but to ease one into a physical and mental connection with their partner. It has really played out that way in every aspect of our relationship. We've savored the time we spend together since day one. I love that I can just get aroused looking into your eyes."

Michael had touched a nerve in Felicia, she began to cry. Through her tears she began to speak. "I never told anyone this. As much as I loved Adrian, there were times he would physically abuse me when it came to lovemaking. He was into role playing and because of my love for him, I allowed myself to be submissive to his fantasies. I questioned him about it and maybe it was my naivety that kept me believing it was okay when he responded that it was perfectly normal behavior for married couple to experiment."

Michael rose up from the bath and took Felicia into his arms. As he wrapped a towel around her, he assured her she would never have to worry again about feeling uncomfortable in a physical relationship with him. "You give me everything I need sweetheart. You know what appeases me and you always seem so comfortable in everything you do. Look at how we came to love each other. It was all about acceptance and communication. We have never been afraid to talk to one another."

It had been awhile since Michael felt emotional but as he had touched upon something in Felicia, her story touched upon something in him.

"There are so many similarities between us Felicia. While in everyone's eyes it looked like Melanie and I were the perfect couple, we did not have much of a physical relationship. I wanted to blame myself for working long hours but the little time we had together there seemed to be something missing. A few days after I got my divorce papers, I received a call from a friend of mine who heard about Melanie and I breaking up. He said he had known for quite some time that Melanie was spending time with Robbie Banco while I was putting in all those hours. I told him that I had known they were friends even before she and I met. Still, in my heart I knew Melanie would never be unfaithful. She even told me in her letter about her friendship with him and how the divorce would let her be free to be with him. All's well that ends well because now we are together to live our life, loving one another the way we always wanted to be loved." Michael untucked the towel from Felicia's waist and pulled her warmed body into his. She wrapped her arms around his neck and raised her lips to meet his. "I love you Michael."

"I love you too, Felicia." Michael said as he kissed her.

Chapter 21

Jade and Romance

Jade and Romance

Michael took Felicia's hand and led her with the gift she had given him into the bedroom.

As the two sat facing one another on the bed wrapped in fresh, dry towels, Michael told Felicia to close her eyes. He handed her the small box and told her to open her eyes. Inside was the jade necklace he had gotten for his grandmother. When she passed from this earth, his aunt sent it to him. He unlatched the hook and placed it around Felicia's neck. "This has always held a special place in my heart. I brought this for my grandmother for her 75th birthday. She promised it would come back to me if anything ever happened to her. She is looking down on us right now, smiling. I know you would have loved her and she the same with you."

As Felicia rubbed her hands across the stones, she looked at Michael and said. "Just like the song, *You Make Me Feel Brand New.*"

"Okay honey, now it's time for you to open your gift." Michael reached over and pulled the box onto his lap. He pulled the top off and unwrapped the tissue paper to reveal a pair of white silk pajamas. As ran his hand across the fabric he looked over to the chaise lounge next to the bed where Felicia had hung the blouse she wore at dinner.

Without saying a word, he got up and retrieved the silk garment, placed it over Felicia's shoulders and asked her to put it on. "What an incredible turn on it was for me sitting at the table with you wearing this. I was fantasizing about you while you were getting ready for me to come up."

Felicia rose up from the bed, took the draped towel off and walked into the bathroom with the silk garment slung across one shoulder. As she entered, she spun around revealing her firm, naked body, swirled the blouse around her head and spoke. "It will be my extreme pleasure to put this on for you, now if you would put on your new gift as well and oh, that incredible cologne okay?"

"Will be back in a flash, I need to go get it." Michael said.

Felicia pointed to the far corner of the room. "No need to dear. Hope you don't mind, I happened to see it as I passed your old room sitting on the bed and took the liberty of putting it on top of my vanity so you could put it on after our bath." As she turned back, she blew Michael a kiss and slipped behind the glass door. The feel of the silk against his shaved body felt so smooth. Michael's sandalwood cologne mixed well with Felicia's spiced fragrance leaving an erotically pleasant air in the room.

Felicia reappeared wearing the white silk blouse. Her lips were painted a silvery high gloss sheen with metallic silver eye shadow to match the highlights in her hair. She had slipped into a pair of shimmering, sheer pantyhose under the now completely unbuttoned blouse. As she walked towards the bed the dimmed light from the bathroom reflected across her body giving it an effervescent glow.

Michael stood up, held out his hand and eased her back onto the bed.

She sat upright facing him in a lotus position. He reached out and pulled her onto his lap and wrapped her legs around his waist. The two sat there gazing silently into one another's eyes. The passion that began in the bath had never subsided.

With his hands firmly wrapped around her waist, Michael drew her moistened lips to his. As he pulled away, Felicia parted her mouth and ran her tongue over Michael's lips just enough to taste them. As she pulled back, Michael released his hands from her waist, eased her blouse down past her shoulders and ran his fingertips up and down her back. Felicia was getting more and more aroused and pushed Michael gently back onto the bed. She stayed atop him looking down into his eyes as she edged her blouse off. He reached up and cupped her breasts in his hands.

Michael just laid there looking at the firmness of her stomach muscles as she arched herself backwards, his own passion intensifying as kissed her breasts, now erect from his touches. With each kiss, Felicia could feel her insides shivering as she arched upright, placing her hands on, Michael's chest, she began gently rocking back and forth. Her movement across the silk was extremely pleasurable for them.

She reached down and pulled at his shorts until they were past his buttocks. As Michael raised his hips up to help her, Felicia, pushed herself into him. As she did, they gripped one another's hands. Michael pulled Felicia towards him. She unbuttoned his top, put her arms around him and began kissing him. As her lips and tongue rolled over the crevice of his neck, Felica could feel Michael's arousal against her inner thighs. He raised his knees upright and pushed her back against his legs.

Unfolding, was everything they had discussed regarding their Kama Sutra teachings about intimacy. The way they looked at one another as if they were able to see into their souls. The erotic exchange of those slow, soft kisses that let them explore and taste the sweetness of every inch of their flesh.

Though they had both experienced lovemaking in a long relationship with other partners, there was a redefining and rebirth with everything they shared on this night. The meaning of love became a way life in every moment to be shared not just, in bed.

They knew from how they had abstained until this evening that the gentle caressing of their fingertips could enlighten their senses for hours. What created such intensity between them was Michael's ability to time and control his release while Felicia used her training as a way of controlling her stomach and pelvic muscles to ensure an even heightened experience.

As they made love, they stared into one another's eyes with an almost submissive gaze. The slow, gentle back and forth motion brought Felicia to heights of pleasure she had never known before. Michael felt himself melt into her.

Felicia put her lips up to his ear and whispered to him about the tingling sensations she felt reverberating between their naked bodies. "The beautifulness of you inside me honey, oh my God, such intense, emotional climaxes, I had to bite my lips."

As she communicated her pleasure, Michael responded by turning her over on her back and gently positioning himself on top of her. He began giving her feather soft kisses on her neck and shoulders and easing himself in and out of her.

As he made love to her again, Felicia pulled her lips up to meet his, pulled back and said. "Michael, I want you to let yourself completely go." With that, Felicia pulled the jade necklace up to her pursed lips and held the beads in between them. As he began to fill her, Michael let out a long, deep moan.

Felicia pressed her lips tightly around the beads and nestled his head against her bosom. She could feel his heart beating in her chest as he lifted his head to her and spoke.

"Look at us love, both in our fifties and sharing what we just did."

As they lay side by side, Michael reached out and took Felicia's hand in his. She turned on her side, tucked her head on his chest and lifted her chin up and kissed him. They both looked over at the candles still flickering through the stain glassed door and laughed before drifting off to sleep.

What a way to end their first "real" night together.

Chapter 22

The English Countryside

The English Countryside

It was close to midday. Felicia and Michael had fallen asleep in one another's arms. As the sun began peering through the sheer curtains, the warm rays fell upon their naked bodies, easing their eyes open. Michael looked down and began running his fingers through Felicia's sun-drenched hair. "Good morning honey."

Felicia tilted her head slightly upward to meet Michael's smiling face. As she did, he bent down and kissed her on the forehead. 'What a beautiful, romantic and fulfilling night sweetheart." She said to him.

"Pure heaven my love, pure heaven." He responded.

As they lay side by side, looking up at the sun-splashed ceiling, the phone rang. Felicia picked it up and looked at the number. It was not an area code she recognized right away but knew it was an overseas exchange. "I wonder who this could be Michael." She said with a grin on her face.

"Hello." Felica spoke into the phone.

"Well, good morning my dear, Jerry Bristol calling."

"Pops, it's so wonderful to hear your voice." She said excitedly.

In the background she could hear Manning. "Be sure to tell that lovely young lady how grateful I am for all she has done to bring you back into my life." Jerry handed Manning the phone.

"Hello dear, life has been wonderful and all because of you. Jerry wanted to call to tell you something special, I know he is anxious. Here he is, love to you, hope to see you in the English countryside one day." Manning gave the phone back to Jerry.

"Felicia, Manning and I have been talking about getting married." Jerry continued.

Felicia put her phone on speaker so Michael could listen in.

"I plan on spending the rest of my life with her and staying here." He went on. "Anyway, we would love for you to come and be a part of our celebration. I know you would love it. We are far removed from city life here in the English countryside with all its quaintness, peace and quiet. Manning and I will take care of your flight and of course, you will have your own room here, just think of it as an English bed and breakfast." He said with that hearty laugh Felicia loved.

Felicia looked over at Michael. Through her happiness, tears were beginning to fall. Michael took her hand in his looked her in the eyes and nodded his head up and down as if to say. *"Yes, let's go."*

"Of course, we will be there, when will it take place Pops?" Felicia asked.

"We, and who is the other part of your life honey?" Jerry asked with a fatherly tone in his voice. "I hope it is that chap I met, Michael, wasn't it?"

"You remembered." Felicia cried.

"How could I ever forget. Jerry said. "He truly put the life back in you. Felicia, you were always like a daughter to me. All I ever wanted was to see you happy and enjoying life again."

"I am so happy, Pops." Felicia's voice softened as Michael wiped the tears of joy from her cheek.

Jerry continued talking about the wedding plans. As he was telling Felicia about the simplicity of his life with Manning, Jerry drifted back to a scene he'd written about in his journal that took place when he first arrived.

"By midmorning, the sun had begun to warm the quaint row houses along the cobblestone street. Manning and I headed out the door and walked towards the meadows toting a blanket and basket filled with food for our afternoon picnic.

We made our way down the street to a path leading onto the hillside. The heavens were filled with white, fluffy clouds hanging from a brilliant, blue sky.

We came to a clearing atop one of the lush, wild-flower filled hills. I opened the blanket and spread it out upon the soft grass. Sitting down, we kicked off our sandals and gazed across the meadows to the other side of the hilltop.

My dear Manning looked exquisite as always. She wore a pale, yellow flowing summer dress with a wide, straw bonnet. Me, the simple man I am, dressed in tan, baggy pants and a white cotton button down shirt.

As we ran through the flowered fields smiling and laughing, the hills sprung to life around us. The tall grass swayed in the gentle breeze as rainbows of wildflowers reached for the warmth in the afternoon sun.

To look at us, one would not think of the many years that had kept us apart. We are a youthful and vibrant picture of love.

As we held hands and danced our way back, I looked over at Manning and said. "My dear, life is truly eternal when love is the nectar in the fountain from which one drinks. I have been able to stay so young at heart just dreaming of you."

"Pops, when is this joining of two hearts taking place?"

Jerry drifted back into the phone conversation with Felicia. "Well dear, it has been a year since I left San Francisco. We want to get married in the meadow where we had our first picnic." Jerry paused. "April is only five weeks away will that be enough time for you and Michael to do what you need to do to be here?"

Felicia laughed. "Pops, do you remember my assistant, Jackie?"

The little feisty one?" He responded.

"I put her in charge of the company to free myself up so I can enjoy my time with Michael and travel for pleasure instead of business. We will be there." She told him.

Michael reached over, took Felicia's hand in his, kissed it and acknowledged the trip with a nod of his head.

"Manning will be so thrilled and so will I to have you here in the English countryside." With that, Jerry said. "Until then, love you." As he hung up the phone.

As they approached the cargo area, Felicia noticed a man holding up a sign with bold, capital letters bearing the name, STOUFFER. She walked up to the neatly dressed lad as if to inquire if London had more than one citizen bearing her name. The chauffeur shook his head, grinned while motioning to the baggage captain.

As the sleek motorcar moved away from the terminal, Michael and Felica, kept their eyes affixed to one another without saying a word.

Passing through London's congested streets, they headed north along the roadway leading to the outskirts of the city. The driver glanced back in his mirror and smiled. "They are a picture of contentment." As Michael and

Felicia glanced out the window, their driver turned his head slightly towards them and spoke. "Tales have it that a noted English poet met and fell in love with the lady of his dreams on a midsummer's night somewhere near here."

Admiring the lush green forests and deep rolling hills. Michael couldn't help but to envision the great writer and his lady riding side by side on their mounts. "It is truly a picturesque place, he shared, one I imagine could inspire many a poetic phrase."

Two hours later, winding through rolling hills and flower filled meadows, they reached a small village outside of London known as, Kingstanding.

Manning lived in one of the brick row houses that lined the cobblestone street of the village. These dwellings had been built with such great care and craftsmanship, their exteriors stood unscathed some three hundred years later.

Many of the interiors had undergone changes to keep up with the times. The original brick walls, hardwood flooring and wooden beam rafters were kept intact. Although many of the fireplaces had been replaced with more modern means of heating, Manning had kept her original hearth.

To see the village in person, one can just close their eyes and imagine, snuggling under a blanket on long, cold wintry nights, with the flickering of firelight dancing across the small four-paned leaded glass windows that framed the quaint two-story row house. Summer evenings were often cool enough in this part of the English countryside which afforded Manning the use of her hearth throughout most of the year.

"A favorite book, a hot cup of tea, some fresh home-made biscuits, yes, the simple things." Felicia envisioned as she thought about Jerry and Manning's nights together.

As the car pulled up to the front door, Manning and Jerry were waiting with open arms to greet their guests.

Felicia ran to Jerry and wrapped her arms around him. "Pops, I can't believe I am here with you." The silver haired gent put his arms on her shoulders and turned her around, Manning was waiting to hug her.

While the two embraced and shed a few tears, Michael and Jerry took the luggage into the house. Manning and Felicia followed.

As they entered the doorway, Michael looked over to the left. Just beyond the parlor doors was the home's original stone fireplace. Michael took Felicia's hand and led her into the parlor.

"Such a cozy way to spend the evening, honey." He said smiling as they made their way to the open hearth.

Manning was right behind them. She placed a fresh log over the iron grate, sprinkled some kindling around it and struck a match. As the fire began to take, Manning reached for Felicia's hand and led her towards the staircase. Michael picked up the luggage and followed.

The brick walls leading up to the second floor were tastefully decorated with the tapestries, quilts and framed needlepoints Manning had done over the years. Aside from her diary, reading and taking care of the children, she had become a gifted crafts maker.

Manning spent her years as a nurse taking care of children with terminal illnesses. The words of wisdom she recited to the children throughout her years at the hospital were lovingly sewn into the beauty of her needlepoint art. Felicia and Michael walked slowly, studying each piece of work as they made their way up the stairs.

As they reached the second floor, Manning turned to the right to reveal another side of herself. Michael, being a painter was awe inspired by Manning Osborne's works. Hanging from the walls were oil paintings capturing the landscape and houses they had passed coming into the quaint village. The lush, rolling countryside and all its splendor were there on canvas, captured like a photograph in oils.

Michael turned to Manning took her hand in his and spoke. "Where did you get such a gift to express yourself so?"

Manning beamed as she stood in front of one of the larger paintings. "All my years of waiting for Jerry to return have been filled with nothing but beautiful images of that day." Michael kissed her on the cheek and turned to face a large painting she had done of the flowered hills. He stood there admiring her gift to paint with such realism.

"One day Manning, not too far off, I will envision this painting in my head and capture it on my own canvas." Manning smiled and led them to the door of their room.

A crystal light fixture hanging from the ceiling cascaded into a waterfall of reddened light and splashed across a large oval mirror. The mirror was perched atop a long mahogany dresser. There were fresh wild-flowers in each corner of the room.

As Manning turned to leave the room, she looked at Felicia and Michael and said. "I know you must be tired from your long journey, unpack your things and join us by the fire for some tea and fresh biscuits."

As Manning headed down the stairs, Michael turned to Felicia, took her in his arms and shared a passionate kiss. Felicia pushed him onto the bed and laid on top of him. "We have a lifetime of making beautiful memories. This is just the beginning of what we talked about; travelling, experiencing nature's beauty, discovering new places and sharing it all with good people like Jerry and Manning."

As they put the last piece of their wardrobes away, Felicia closed the drawer and placed the empty baggage in the corner. The two smiled as they headed down the stairs.

The fire was crackling, sending a warm breeze across the open parlor. Jerry had eased himself into the big, soft cushioned sofa. He gestured to Felicia and Michael to join him. Tired from the miles they'd travelled, they both sunk back into the soft brown leather, shut their eyes for a moment, letting the snapping of the wood soothe their tired souls.

Manning entered the room carrying a tray with piping hot tea, warm biscuits and apple butter, a true English nightcap. As she began to pour the brisk tea, Jerry leaned over and cupped a warm biscuit gently in his hand. He placed his other hand around Manning's soft shoulders.

She took the cup and held it to his lips for him to sip. "My dear, I have waited so long to share this moment." she said cradling the precious china.

"It was well worth the wait. No time could have been more perfect than this." Jerry said as he looked over at Felicia and Michael.

As they indulged in Manning's delicious offerings, Felicia looked at Jerry. "Pops, I look at you and Manning, the love you have for one another and I see that in the man sitting next to me." She took Michael's hand in hers as she continued talking. "Through the years, you never lost sight of one another, never had anyone in your hearts but the other. You grew your love over many years, Michael and I are just beginning." She took Jerry's hand in hers.

"Being like a father to me, I want you to know that this man respects me, protects me and loves me. Like Manning is to you, Pops, Michael is my best friend." Felicia took Manning's hand and placed it in Jerry's. "You have shown us that it never is too late to begin a new life. I never thought I would feel this way." She turned to look at Michael. "If this man were to ask me to marry him, I would jump into his arms without hesitation."

Michael looked at Felicia, a tear forming in each eye. "And, I will my love."

The night was growing old and the fire began to fade as Manning pressed herself into Jerry's gentle arms and the two drifted off to sleep.

Felicia and Michael had retreated to their room. As she lay there nestled the way she loved, into his chest, Felicia closed her eyes knowing Michael was as content as her.

The morning sun rose bringing new life to the small village. The rays began to trickle into the parlor. It was six–twenty, forty more minutes and the bells from the grandfather clock would chime.

Manning awoke, reaching for the quilt draped over the sofa, she eased it onto Jerry.

She opened the small window above the sink to let the cool morning breeze into the kitchen. As she began to slice fresh strawberries, a caramel Yorkshire cat made its way purring into the room. The cat was so content to pull up to Manning's feet and plop her fluffy ball of fur onto the floor.

"Good morning gorgeous," Manning cooed. "Would my little girl like something to eat?" The cat rose up from the floor and put her paws on Manning's leg.

She placed a bowl of food and a bowl of milk at her feet as the morning bird's melodies echoed across the yard through the open window. Manning began to hum along.

On the table, which was adorned with fresh cut flowers from her garden, Manning placed a bowl of fresh strawberries, four bowls of shredded wheat cereal, a pot of tea, some fresh baked brown bread and molasses.

The sound of Manning's voice, the birds singing and the smell of the bread awakened Jerry. He got up and strolled into the kitchen. Manning was standing by the sink with her back towards him. He eased up behind her and gently slid his arms around her waist.

"Good morning love," he said softly as he turned her around and planted a gentle kiss on her lips.

"I would have to say looking out the window, feeling the warm morning breeze and hearing the birds sing, it is quite a lovely day for a picnic."

Michael and Felicia had heard Manning's lovely voice and made their way down to the kitchen.

As the two couples sat at the table, Manning and Jerry shared the stories of their lives.

Although, Felicia had known about the woman Jerry loved, she never knew where it all began.

Jerry began his story. "God works in ways we don't always understand. The life Manning and I had was part of His plan and that plan brought us together after all these years."

Manning shared her part saying she and Jerry met at the tender age of eight growing up on the dungy streets of Liverpool, England. England had fallen into a deep depression, leaving many families too poor to care for their children. Jerry and Manning were orphaned by those hard times.

Jerry sat quietly as Michael and Felicia listened to the story.

"When the Child Labor movement began in England at the end of the nineteenth century, we were part of the thousands of orphaned children sent aboard ships to North America to be taken in and given a new home by families. Upon reaching the shores of Saint John, New Brunswick, Canada where we hoped to be adopted and start a new life together, we were separated. Alone, Jerry and I carried on never burying our dream of being together again." Manning paused to take a sip of her tea.

"Many children were put on farms as free labor. Those who did make it into private homes were often subjected to labor within those households; cleaning, cooking, doing laundry and taking care of the family's younger children while their older ones were away at school."

I was one of the unlucky ones, adopted by an abusive man whose wife had died, leaving him to raise their five children alone. Richard Burkson was a Professor of Engineering at a prestigious university, a man tormented by guilt over the death of his wife. He turned to alcohol to help him cope with the loss. His wife had died of pneumonia, leaving him to take care of their five children. That was where I came in. I bore seven years of this man's abuse for the sake of the children". As tears welled up in her eyes, Jerry put his arm around her. Manning went on.

"As Richard Burkson lay on his death bed, he tried to redeem himself by remembering me in his will.

In the lawyer's office two months after he left this earth, I opened an envelope bearing my name. In the envelope was a check for twenty thousand dollars.

Attached to the check was a letter. Manning began to read the letter she had saved all these years.

"Dear Manning,

When you read this, I will be gone from your life. The many years of pain you have suffered may never be erased by this money, but it was the only way I knew to show you how sorry I was for all I put you through.

When my wife died, I began to submerge myself into a world of anger and hate, my drinking pushed me deeper into that hell. I am certain you will see to it that my youngest has the same love and guidance to help her make her own way as well.

Please take this check and make a life for yourself. Try to understand, I was a man haunted by my own evils. I never meant to harm you or the children.

As I bid farewell, I pray the Lord will be able to redeem all I have done so that all those evils may finally be put to rest.

Goodbye and God Bless You Always, Richard."

Manning folded the letter carried it over to the sink and lit a match to it. She returned to the table, stood behind Jerry, wrapped her arms around him, looked up at Felicia and Michael and finished her story.

"I eventually returned to school and got my degree in nursing. Shortly after, I returned to England, took a job in a small hospital outside of Kingstanding and used what monies I had left over to put a down payment on this house."

She kissed Jerry on the cheek, smiled and said. "I made amends, my past is now buried."

Jerry had his own story to tell. "My life went in a different direction, I was one of the more fortunate ones. I was adopted by a family from Moncton, New Brunswick. Gordon and Lillian Cadbury had immigrated to Canada from England in 1905. The couple never had any children of their own, I filled that void."

The Cadburys were well off. Gordon's family built a shipping empire in England trading teas and spices imported from the Far East.

Jerry had a very good life. He was surrounded by riches but never lost sight of his simple ways. He was a hard-working young man determined to make his own way.

He continued. "Unlike Manning, I had love and respect from my new family. At the age of eighteen, I realized the time had come for me to set out on my own. "Young man," he recalled Gordon Cadbury telling him. "Always treat people with the same respect you have shown Lillian and I and you will never have to worry about being successful."

The man I called Dad told me, New York is the place dreams are made of. He referred me to a friend of his at the Park Place Hotel named Joshua Congdon.

Felicia intervened. "Pops, isn't that the father of Jason, the man who owns the Bristol Building?" "Yes, my dear, it is." Jerry went on. "I wore a dark blue wool suit. Hanging from my pocket was a shiny gold chain attached to a gold pocket watch my Dad had given me. He had slipped ten crisp $100 bills into my hand as I boarded the train to New York."

He reached over and took Manning's hand in his. "That first job I had was the start of something that lasted a lifetime. It took me from New York to San Francisco back to my homeland."

"Jerry, your life and Manning's life are a story to be told. I would love one day to be able to capture it in a book." Michael stated.

Felicia put her arm around Michael's shoulder and beamed. "If it wasn't for Michael wanting to write a book, we may never have met."

"How true honey, how true." Michael responded.

Manning and Jerry made plans with Felicia and Michael to go on a picnic and show them were they were going to exchange their vows.

By midmorning, the sun had begun to warm the quaint row houses along the cobblestone street.

The two couples headed out the door and walked towards the meadows toting a blanket and basket filled with food for their afternoon picnic. They made their way down the street to a path leading onto the hillside. The heavens were filled with white, fluffy clouds hanging from a brilliant, blue sky. They came to a clearing atop one of the lush, wild-flower filled hills.

Jerry opened the blanket and spread it out upon the soft grass. Sitting down, all of them kicked off their sandals and gazed across the meadows to the other side of the hilltop.

Manning Osborne looked exquisite as always. She wore a flowered summer dress with a straw bonnet. Jerry was dressed in his usual baggy pants and a white cotton button down shirt. Felicia and Michael were dressed in white cotton drawstring pants with black matching button down shirts.

Jerry and Manning led the way as they all walked barefoot through the fields. They were smiling and laughing as the hills sprung to life around them. The tall grass swayed in the gentle breeze as rainbows of flowers reached for the warmth in the afternoon sun.

They arrived back at the picnic site and sat down on the soft quilt. Manning took Felicia's and Michael's hands in hers and said. "This is the very spot we had our first picnic when Jerry first arrived and tomorrow, we will be wed here."

Chapter 23

The Journal and The Painting

The Journal and The Painting

Sunday was upon them. Atop the hillside, Manning and Jerry stood face to face, with Felicia and Michael at their sides as they exchanged their vows.

Manning looked more beautiful than ever in an ankle length white lace dress accented by a pale yellow wide brimmed bonnet. She accented her dress with the yellow beaded bracelet and necklace Jerry had given her as a wedding present. The groom was dressed in white linen pants with a pale, yellow button down, shirt.

There was no minister, at this stage in their lives, Jerry and Manning trusted God's blessing as they read their promises of love to one another.

Jerry looked into Manning's eyes and spoke softly. "I have counted the minutes, hours and days. I have watched the weeks go by and shorn the months from my calendar as they passed. The seasons have changed but our love for one another remained. I wish to spend the rest of my days cherishing, loving and taking care of you." He pulled her hands up to his lips and kissed them. He placed his hands on each side of her face, looked into her watery eyes and asked. "Will you walk with me for all those days?"

A tear fell upon his fingers. Manning raised the teardrop to her lips and said. "I will walk all of those days with you, my love."

Manning recited her vow. "I waited ever so patiently for that time I would see you again, for that time when I could spend my life with you, to love, cherish and take care of you." Manning took Jerry's hands in hers and asked. "Will walk with me and let me love, cherish and take care of you for all of my days?"

Felicia and Michael looked across at one another., tears were falling for them as well.

Jerry placed an "African Violet", tanzanite and diamond ring, the color of Manning's eyes on her finger. "Yes, my darling, I will walk with you for all of those days."

As the ceremony came to an end, Felicia and Michael hugged and congratulated the newlyweds. The couples danced barefoot in the wildflower covered fields to Manning's voice as she sang, "The Sound of Music."

Back at the house, Manning and Felicia had everything ready for a simple but elegant celebration. The mood was set in the den with classical music and a crackling fire. After the couples finished toasting their friendship and good fortune for the love in their lives, Manning excused herself and headed upstairs. She returned holding a rectangular package wrapped in plain, brown paper.

"Jerry and I wanted you to have this as a keepsake not only of this momentous occasion but as a memory of your time here. As Felicia carefully undid the wrapping, the painting she and Michael had admired when they first arrived was unveiled. "This will hang in our home right above the fireplace." Felicia said. Jerry then got up and went into the kitchen. He came back holding a small package wrapped in the same brown paper and handed it to Michael.

"Manning felt it was time to close this chapter on her life and wanted to pass it on to you. It is the journal she kept when she first arrived in Canada. Perhaps when you sit down to write your book, this journal will find its way as one of those publications."

Michael ran his hands across the lettering on the covering. *"Manning Osborne of Kingstanding."*

"I already have it in my head." He replied.

Manning would be returning to the hospital tomorrow and invited Felicia and Michael to join her and Jerry as she made her rounds in the children's ward. "It will be a very enlightening experience for both of you." She said.

"We would love to." Felicia replied.

As the momentous day came to an end and the fire's embers began to fade, the newly wedded couple lay asleep in one another's arms. Felicia took the quilt from the back of the sofa and placed it across them. Michael held the painting and journal as he and Felicia made their way up to their room.

Song birds had perched themselves on the windowsill at the break of dawn. Felicia opened her eyes and looked up at Michael. "Good morning darling, what a heavenly way to be awakened." Michael wrapped his arms around her. "Indeed, it is my love." Felicia said as she wrapped her fingers into his hand.

They held hands and skipped down the stairs like little kids as the smell of fresh baked molasses bread filled the air. As they waltzed into the kitchen, Jerry was sitting at the table reading the paper while Manning was humming along with the birds, preparing breakfast. "Good morning Pops." Felicia said. "Well Good Morning my dear." Jerry responded as he rose up to receive Felicia's hug.

As they were hugging Jerry looked over her shoulder at Michael then back to her.

"So, my dear Felicia, when will we have the pleasure of seeing the two of you join hands?" Manning turned around to hear Felicia's response. "Is next

Summer good for you Michael?" She said blowing him a kiss. "Perfect my love." He reciprocated, blowing her a kiss back.

Just like she had said. *"A very enlightening experience."* As they walked into the children's ward at the hospital, Michael and Felicia saw just what captured Manning's heart.

"What a gift of love and compassion this woman has." Michael thought to himself, seeing the children's eyes light up as Manning walked into the room.

Manning whispered in Michael's ear and pointed over to the corner of the room. He picked up a book of poems, sat down in the center of the room and began reading aloud. The boys and girls circled around him listening attentively as each word flowed from his lips. Felicia felt herself being drawn even closer in love. As she watched him engage the boys and girls, her eyes teared up.

At one point, Michael looked from the book at Manning. As he watched her holding a little boy dying of cancer, he began to see that life held more for him than writing a book. He swallowed hard as the reality of a small child's pains stared back at him from the eyes of a four-year-old.

All these years he had been afraid of being a father. He reached out and took Felicia's hand and sat her on his lap as he continued reading. The children were all smiles. One little boy laughed and said. "Give her a kiss Mr. Michael." He did just that.

When he finished reading, Michael led Felicia over to the big picture window. Looking out on to the courtyard, he studied his and Felicia's reflection in the glass. Closing his eyes for a moment, he began to say a prayer of thanks for all the goodness life had blessed him with. He asked God to heal the little boy who now lay sleeping in Manning's arms.

As Michael turned to look at Felicia, the morning sun warmed the side of his face. With the brush of her hand, Felicia wiped a tear from his cheek.

Always afraid about being a father, those fears were now gone from Michael's life.

Tuesday morning arrived quickly. Michael and Felicia bid their farewells to Manning and Jerry. "Don't forget." As they all hugged, "You have a wedding to attend next Summer."

Chapter 24

"You Are So Beautiful, To Me"

"You Are So Beautiful, To Me"

The transatlantic flight arrived on time in San Francisco. As they made their way to the baggage carousel, Michael couldn't help but think back to the day he walked this same path with Felicia's arm tucked in his as she scanned the crowd looking for Cal.

Oh, how times had changed. Michael would be the one driving them home now.

"You know honey, last time we made this trip from the airport, I was asking Cal to drop me off at the office. Not this time, we have five days all to ourselves and we are going to have some fun." Felicia said glancing over from the mirror as she refreshed her makeup.

Michael looked over and said. "Let's stop at the market and get some nice, juicy steaks. The weather's just right for grilling. We could take our wine out on the patio and dine under the stars. How's that for kicking off our homecoming?"

"A nice juicy steak with baked potato and that fabulous Malbec from Argentina we adore and all under the stars with the man I love, now's that's what I call, heavenly bliss." Felicia reached over, took Michael's hand and wrapped it around her shoulder as she leaned in and kissed him on the cheek.

The owners of The Sausalito Market loved seeing their favorite couple. There weren't too many who shared the passion for gourmet cooking like they did. There was an instant connection the first time Michael and Felicia walked in. As the other shoppers took notice of this handsome couple, so did Sasha and Kim Lee.

The two women, now in their forties, had immigrated from Seoul, Korea to attend culinary school in Sacramento. Knowing how expensive and competitive it was to launch a new restaurant in the Bay area, they decided to open a gourmet market to cater to chefs. The woman prided themselves on offering the best in everything they carried from fruits and vegetables to the cuts of meat and fish right down to the unique imported spices.

They hosted cooking classes on Saturdays and provided customers with daily recipes that listed not only the meals ingredients but, the recommended wine to accompany the dish. They were clever marketers as well, something Felicia appreciated being in the advertising business, in that they had the cost of the meal per person tallied at the bottom of the recipe/item list. This was Sasha's and Kim's ticket to success along with their superb selection of wines.

When Felicia and Michael came in, Sasha and Kim would rush over and hug them. They confessed to Felicia one day that they had a crush on Michael but not to worry because they could never hold a candle to her. Felica felt complimented as she ribbed Michael. "Sweetheart, why do you think they pay so much attention to you when we go there. Don't you see them getting all dreamy eyed?" Michael just smiled and kept pushing the cart.

"It's so good to be home." Felicia remarked as they pulled through the gate. As much as they loved the quaint and quiet countryside of England, they both agreed, being back in San Francisco was more conducive to their lifestyle. Neither one of them could wait to get through the door, shower and put on comfy clothes. It had been quite the trip and they both needed the extra five days to unwind.

Michael had a special recipe planned for the grilled steaks. He would season them and cook them on a high flame *"Pittsburgh style"* which was, the blackening or crusting of the outside, searing in the juices, leaving the insides a nice, tender rare to medium rare. "Chef Boy-O-Boy", as Felicia loved to call him knew the perfect steak would take about 3-4 minutes on each side using an intense flame from an open-hearth oven which was exactly what she had custom built on her deck.

Before pulling off the steaks, Michael would spread Danish blue cheese and cracked pepper over the top with a layer of asparagus, to give them a flavor to die for. And of course, with this scrumptious meal would be Felicia's favorite, a baked potato with chives, bacon and sour cream. The Malbec would be the perfect accompaniment.

As Michael manned the grill, Felicia sat at the table admiring him. She thought about how hard working and talented he was. He was so romantic, could cook extraordinary meals, write incredibly and although she hadn't experienced it with him yet, she pictured him being a great painter as well.

As Felicia sat at the table sipping her wine, Michael raised his glass and blew her a kiss. He thought about her strong work ethics and how she rose from relative obscurity to one of the top advertising firms in the country. Another part of Felicia that Michael admired was how she could go from being a savvy, business women one minute to a playful lover the next. He loved how comfortable he felt with her no matter what they were doing, where they were or who they were with.

As they sat at the table enjoying being home, their conversation centered around the children they engaged with at the hospital in England.

"Honey, I have to admit." Michael began. "Until we went to visit those children, I always feared being a father. It wasn't so much about fatherhood but if I would be able to dedicate my life raising an extension of me."

"What do you mean Michael, you are such a loving and giving person." Felica said to him compassionately. "I watched you engage those kids, you brought smiles to their faces. As you read to them, their eyes lit up. Michael, I don't know if you realize the impact you make on people with your presence and energy, there is something that just emanates from within you that fills people with positive energy. I know firsthand what I am talking about. I felt it from the moment I sat next to you on the plane." She reached out and took hold of Michael's hands.

"When we were in England, I was afraid that my mind would be consumed by the death of Adrian, that I would want to seek out where he was buried and kneel in front of him." Instead of tears which could have so easily fallen recalling what had transpired over four years ago, Felicia was at ease and smiling. "I never shared this but, Adrian always told me that when he died, his wish was to be buried next to his grandmother. He did not want to be mentioned in the papers, nor did he want any celebration of his life, Adrian just wanted me to make sure his wish was fulfilled and, that's exactly what I did".

Michael reached his arm around Felicia. "My darling, I too wondered if being in England would be hard for you, but you never, ever showed me or Jerry and Manning anything but love and happiness."

"I know now, with you by my side that I have someone who compliments me. I promise you this my love, you and I will have children in our lives first though, we need to begin planning our wedding."

Felicia jumped out of her chair and took Michael's hand. "Let's dance as if it were our wedding day."

The starburst clock was now sitting at 10:28. It had been seventeen hours since they arose for the journey back to San Francisco. Neither one of them showed any signs of jet lag. They carried the dishes to the sink and stood side by side as always, one washing, the other drying.

"We have five more days to ourselves." Michael said. "I thought we could go to the museum one day, the theater another and guess what I came up with while we were eating?"

"What honey?" Felicia asked.

"On our way home, we passed the signs leading to Giants stadium. How would you like to go to a baseball game?"

Felicia pulled back from their dance and made like she was standing on the pitcher's mound with a runner on first. She veered in for the signs from the catcher, pulled her imaginary glove up to her face, looked over at first to make sure the runner was not going to try and steal and went into a wind up. Teasingly, she threw the ball to Michael who had now crouched down to retrieve her throw.

"Steeeeeerike." He shrilled while making a loud popping noise as if Felicia had just blazed a ninety-seven mile an hour fastball past the batter.

Felicia jumped for joy. "Oh. Honey, I would love to go to a game. I love baseball. As, long as I have lived here, I have never been to a live one."

Really, you have never been to a game?" Michael asked.

"Never." Felicia replied.

"Hot dogs and beer and, of course the seventh inning stretch with, *take me out to the ballgame.*" Michael began to sing the song.

With the plans for a fun few days made, Felicia and Michael headed upstairs.

"Would you join me in the shower my love?" Felicia said seductively.

"An invitation I dare not pass up." Michael said as he patted Felicia on the backside.

As they stood under the steaming hot jets, Felicia handed Michael a loofa saturated with a peppermint scented liquid soap. "My muscles are really tired from sitting upright on that plane for so long, care to massage them for me with this?" Michael obliged and turned Felica's back to him. Taking the sponge into his hand, he applied soft, circular motions with the lather up and down her back. As he did, he could sense Felicia's pleasure as she titled her head back and kissed him on the neck. He reached around to her stomach and ran his hand across her arms. Felicia extended her arms outward as Michael ran the loofa across her stomach and up over her breasts.

Felicia took the sponge from Michael and reciprocated. She turned him around and pushed her hips into him as she rolled the soapy lather up and down the back of his body. As the mint eased into their pores, they both felt a tingling sensation.

The soft touches. The minty lather. "Yes, oh yes, honey." Felicia shrilled as she not only reached her own climax but brought Michael to one with the lather. They stood there spent with the steaming water cascading upon them.

Michael looked at Felicia and pulled her to him and began to sing. *"You are so beautiful, to me."*

As they lay in bed drifting off to slumber land Michael looked over at Felicia. "Ever been to McCovey's Cove?"

"No, but it sounds like a great place to have a picnic." Felica replied.

Michael smiled and kissed her as they both drifted off to sleep.

Chapter 25

McCovey's Cove

"What a beautiful day for a ballgame." Michael said as he leaned over and kissed Felicia good morning. They both slipped into casualwear of sweats and sneakers then headed downstairs for a light breakfast of coffee, bagels with cream cheese and a fruit cup.

"You are in for quite the experience." Michael gleamed as he got out the cooler, baseball mitts and tanning lotion. For the end of April, it was an unusually warm day in the Bay area. The temperatures would reach eighty degrees with clear skies and sunshine abundant.

"Honey." Michael said as they headed out the gate past the totem poles. "Thought we could stop by the market and pick up some cheese, grapes, a fresh loaf of sourdough bread and of course it will all be shared with, thou."

"What about the hot dogs and beer honey?" Felicia asked. "At the stadium, my love." Michael replied.

"Well, good morning lovebirds." Sasha greeted them with exuberance as they entered the market. "How was the trip to England?"

"Absolutely incredible." Felicia exclaimed. "The wedding was one out of a fairytale. A lush English countryside bursting with lavender and wildflowers. It was just the bride and groom, Michael and I, so simple yet elegant." Michael chimed in. "The whole experience was amazing. After the ceremony, the bride sang the title song from, *"The Sound of Music"* as we whirled and danced barefoot through the tall grass. It really solidified so many things about living life simply, just basking in God's natural wonderments."

Just then Kim appeared holding a bottle of champagne. "To, my lovely friends, our gift to you to celebrate your own nuptials."

"But we weren't the ones to tie the knot Kim." Michael said.

"I know." Kim responded. "But, do you not see it in your future?"

Michael looked over at Felicia, smiled and looked back at Kim and Sasha. "We do, yes, we do and you, will be there to join in our special day."

In their hearts, Michael and Felicia knew, in a little over a year, they would be exchanging their vows and all their friends would be there to celebrate with them. Cal and Candice, Jerry and Manning and of course, Sasha and Kim.

They arrived at the stadium well before game time. The parking lot was already filling up with tailgaters as they parked the Rover. Michael ran around to open the door for Felicia. He extended his hand and eased her out into his arms. "Are you ready to enjoy America's pastime sweetheart." Michael asked.

"With you, I am always ready, my dear." Felicia said excitedly.

Michael pulled the filled cooler out from the back. Felicia took hold of his arm as he led her across the parking lot towards the stadium. They proceeded along the walkway to the back of the stadium.

Felica seemed to be bewildered. "Aren't we going in?"

Michael had saved the best for last as they made their way towards the dock.

Boats were already anchored in McCovey's Cove as Michael glanced around. Spotting an attendant, he walked over and handed him a print out.

Felicia was still a bit confused but took everything in stride knowing Michael was always full of the extraordinary when it came to their outings.

The attendant led them to a small motorboat docked in bay # 44, Willie McCovey's jersey number during his playing days with the Giants. The dock attendant led them onto the boat, gave Michael brief instructions on operation and safety and pointed over to the side. "There, is your net to scoop up a home run ball." He started the engine and stepped back on to the dock and untied the line.

Felicia still wrestled with the fact that they weren't heading towards their seats inside.

"Honey." Michael said as he maneuvered the small craft out into the calm water. 'I wanted this to be a unique experience for you, so I took the liberty of putting us in the middle of the famous McCovey's Cove.

Now, Felicia understood what McCovey's Cove was.

The designers made the right field line a little over three hundred feet from home plate thus allowing a decent hit ball to exit the stadium and land in the water.

Michael anchored the boat dead center with where he thought they would have the best odds of getting a homerun ball.

"I am feeling lucky today, I think one is going to come our way." He laughed.

"How, will we know when one is hit?" Felicia asked.

"Trust me my love, we will know." Michael replied convincingly.

The boat was equipped with a flat screen television so they could see the game as if they were inside the stadium. Michael turned it on.

"By the way sweetheart, there is a guy that goes around the cove in his boat selling hot dogs and beer so, you will have the favorite food of America's pastime." Michael poked her and laughed.

"Are you serious Michael?" Felicia had a hard time believing this one.

"Honey, see that boat over there?" Michael pointed towards the dock.

"Oh, Michael, talk about ingenuity, the one shaped like the Weiner Mobile." Felicia had seen the best now in having the right idea to make a buck and was laughing hysterically.

In the top of the fourth, there was a loud eruption from the crowd. Michael told Felicia to look up. As she did a ball came sailing over the wall and plunked down about fifty feet from where they were anchored. "*A little too far.*" Michael murmured to himself.

"Wow, that's amazing." Felicia exclaimed as boaters scrambled to get the ball.

As they sat there basking in the sun, delighting themselves with the wine and cheese, the game went on without much fanfare. It was a pitcher's duel from the fourth inning on.

In the bottom of the 8th, another loud roar burst from the crowd. Michael pointed upward as another ball arched up over the stadium. It was heading straight towards them. The ball came down with a splash and bobbled about ten feet away from the back of the boat.

Michael scrambled over, took the net in his hands, leaned over the back of the boat and began fishing the ball out. As the ball drifted away from him, he leaned further over the railing In, an instant, he plunged with the net in his hand, head first into the water.

"Michael!" Felicia screamed. "Are you okay?"

Michael popped up from the water, reached up and clung on to the back of the boat. Soaking wet, he threw the net on to the deck and pulled himself up into the boat. Felicia reached over and grabbed a hold of Michael's dripping sweatshirt and helped him aboard. As he lay sprawled out, puddles of water surrounding him, Felicia kneeled next to him, unbuttoned his shirt, slipped it off, took a towel and began drying him.

As they were huddling on the wet deck, the boat began to rock gently. As it did, a ball rolled out of the net and nestled besides them. As Felica leaned over to kiss Michael's drenched face, he scooped up the ball and handed it to her.

Michael burst out laughing. Felicia couldn't help but join in and the two of them began laughing uncontrollably.

He pulled her tightly on top of him and said with a wink. "I told you, this was our lucky day."

Chapter 26

Shells, Sea Glass, Stones and Driftwood

Shells, Sea Glass, Stones and Driftwood

Spring flew by so quickly. After they returned from England Michael and Felicia spent much of their time talking about their future together. Driving along the coasts of California, Oregon and Washington, they envisioned the perfect setting where they would exchange their vows. They knew their marriage wouldn't take place in a conventional church setting, each of them had been down that road before. The picture drawn in their minds and in their discussions would be someplace outdoors where they could stand amongst their guests in awe of the surroundings. Perhaps, standing cliffside, next to the ocean in Lincoln City, Oregon.

On July 4th weekend, as they shared a glass of wine at The Plymouth Inn, watching the fireworks over the bay, Felicia reminded Michael about the trip they had taken to Lincoln City shortly after Cal left for New York to be with Candice.

"It was after midnight when we arrived. We stopped at this little roadside motel. You asked to look at the room which I am so grateful you did."

Felicia's eyes popped out when the innkeeper opened the door and turned on the light. She nudged Michael and planted her foot on top of his as if to say. *"Let's get the hell out of here!"*

Michael being the gentleman he is thanked the innkeeper and told him the room was a little too small for their four kids, mother and father and three dogs that were right up the road waiting to join them. The innkeeper turned without saying a word and practically ran back to the office. You could hear him lock the door as he pulled the shade and turned on the *"No Vacancy"* sign. As they drove away, Felicia punched Michael in the shoulder lovingly and said. 'Where did you ever come up with a tall tale like. that?" "I couldn't bear to hurt his feelings." Michael grinned to her.

Felicia went on." It was now close to one thirty in the morning and we both figured we'd just look for a twenty-four- hour diner and hang there until the sun began to rise. Lo and behold, you spotted a small, obscure sign on the side of the road saying nothing more than, *"The Inn at The End of The Road"*. You turned at the sign and headed up this dark, dirt road. Remember, how we couldn't see three feet in front of us even with the high beams on, I mean, honey, it was pitch black dark!" Then out of nowhere, pops up this place. There was a sign, all it said was, "Office." Next to it was an old wall lantern shining upon a sidewalk leading downwards."

Michael's face lit up as he recollected what transpired next.

"You waited in the car as I made my way down those steps. As I approached the door to the office, I began to feel a little creepy. It reminded me of the office at, The Bates Motel, you know, the one in the movie <u>Psycho</u>.

So, there I was lightly tapping on the door thinking. *"Here we are out in the middle of God knows where, not a soul around, no light anywhere except the one on the wall and the one at the office.* Just then Michael stopped and began to laugh heartily. "When that guy answered the door, I took one look at him and thought. *"And he even looks like Anthony Perkins character, what did I get us into?"*

Felicia never witnessed that first encounter Michael had. Her part in all of this was this tall thin man in his forties with glasses leading them to the door of their room, unlocking the door and handing them the key before bidding them a goodnight.

What a soft-spoken man he was." Felicia remarked as Michael went on.

As they made their way up the stairs, they saw that this was more of an apartment than a hotel room. There was a living room with a big over stuffed sleeper sofa and a full kitchen. Michael took one look at the couch, pulled out the bed which was clean and neatly made up with white cotton sheets. To the side of the couch was a recliner with a fluffy white cotton down comforter and four pillows. Michael finished off the bed with the comforter and threw the pillows on top.

"Remember the bathroom?" Michael asked. "It had an old claw foot tub and pedestal sink and as tempting as it was, we were so exhausted from driving all day and night, we just washed up with a washcloth, brushed our teeth and plopped down on what was one of the most comfortable sleeper sofas I ever laid in."

"Oh Michael, when our heads hit those pillows under that soft blanket, that was it till sunrise."

And sunrise brought with it, an incredible surprise.

At dawning, a sound that had lulled them into a deep sleep revealed itself. The morning's light was creeping in through a heart shaped cutout on a set of antiquated wooden shutters.

Felicia continued. "We both propped our heads up looked at the shutters and then to one another. You took me by the hand and led me over to them taking the carved handles into your fingers and pulling them ajar to let the sunlight in. We both looked outward, and panned across a reddish, orange sky. There was nothing but sky, no obstructions, no trees, nothing, but a big, beautiful sky." Felicia sighed as she finished her recap of that incredible journey to Lincoln City, Oregon.

That and a flock of soaring and swooping seagulls was all they saw for as far as the eyes could see until, they looked down to discover where that lulling sound was coming from. Three hundred feet below their eyes rested upon the magnificence of nature's beauty.

Waves made their way upon the shore. The rushing onshore, was the sound Michael and Felicia heard throughout the night. There were no rocky barriers, that was why the music the ocean played was unobstructed and soothing, not crashing and turbulent.

They poured themselves fresh cups of coffee and headed down the stairs. Walking outside Michael looked for a pathway that would take them down the cliffside to the beach. Sure enough, in the back of the inn, a jagged, sandy path had been cut out over the years by visitors tamping the grass and ground underfoot, wanting to make their way down the cliffside to experience the beach. Michael and Felicia took that same path and walked in their bare feet for what seemed like miles. Felicia has a jar sitting on her fireplace mantle filled with the shells, sea glass and stones they collected that day. Michael took the ornate piece of driftwood he found, applied a clear coat of varnish and hung it on the wall in his studio.

Another idea for their wedding site included the Okanagan Valley in Canada. Michael and Felicia spent a weekend there when he and Candice were honored by the BC Ministry of Tourism for their magazine articles about the region's vineyards.

Think of it, Michael, it would almost be like the setting for Jerry and Manning's wedding. The terrain is quite different though, the hilltops are lush then sweep down to rugged cliffsides overlooking the lake. It would make for some amazing photography for our album as we have already seen through Candice's work."

Michael thought for a moment then responded. "Sweetheart, I love the fact that we do not have to book a church or reception hall so that pretty much leaves us open to explore many options.

Michael took Felicia's hand in his. "As much as I love the two scenarios we just discussed, we still have some time to make a decision. Something inside just tells me, there is a place you and I have been to and it may have been before we even met, that is destined to be the place we exchange our vows." Felicia digested every word he said but, said nothing. She just squeezed his hand and gave him a soft kiss on the lips and smiled.

Chapter 27

The Children Make an Impact

The Children Make an Impact

Throughout the Summer and Fall, Michael and Felicia were busy with work. They still shared their weekend visits back and forth between Felicia's house and Michael's studio. Saturday mornings were set aside for treasure hunting. They would rise early pack a cooler and head out to new off the beaten path places to find yard sales and thrift stores. If they ventured too far from home, they would nestle down in a quaint bed and breakfast for the evening. Sundays were reserved as a day of meditation and quiet reflection along with the preparation of a delicious, home cooked meal.

One Sunday morning as Michael and Felicia sat out on the deck sipping their coffee, Felicia brought up their experience with the children at the hospital in England.

"From the time I saw how you were with those children Michael, it really put a whole new perspective on us having our own family one day." Michael put his coffee down as Felicia continued. "We are both at a place in life where we have so much to give to those in need. I am not talking about material giving, what I mean is that you and I are in a position to make a difference in the lives of children like the ones we were with at Manning's hospital"

Michael extended his hand and brought Felicia around the table and sat her on his lap. "Tell me more, honey, I think I know where you are going with this, but I want to hear it from your lips before I say anything."

"Missionary work Michael, can you see us going to other countries to work in small villages taking care of kids?" Felicia was compassionate with every word she spoke. "We could take a year or two off after we get married and work as missionaries. Just think of how gratifying and rewarding it would be for us."

"I know you will think, I am just saying this to appease you, but it really is coming from my heart." Felicia held out her hand up to Michael's mouth as if to hush him. "Dear, you will never have to appease me by agreeing with me, if this is something totally out of your realm, just say so."

"Felicia, that morning I read to those children who, could still smile and laugh in spite of all the pains they were going through, I felt like some angelic presence had entered me and opened my heart to what really matters in life." Tears began to fall from his eyes. "When we stood in that window staring out at the courtyard, I was looking at your reflection. I began to feel such an energy with you next to me. I realized in that moment that you and I share a special kind of love that seems to bring happiness into the lives of the people around us no matter what their circumstances are."

"Michael, you radiate with this glow and people pick up on it when you are around them. I never had that until you came into my life. With you it goes beyond being happy, I could say it's more of a positive energy kind of thing. I watch how people light up in your presence." Felicia was making Michael smile with her words.

"Well, you know something honey, you had that light inside you all the time it's just that when we are together, people feel it coming at them from both of us. By the way, contrary to what you might have thought, I welcome the chance to do missionary work because there are so many children out there that we can bring our love to." Michael said warmly.

"Michael, I love your compassion for others." Felicia replied.

In November, Felicia received a text message from Candice.

"I know we haven't spoken for a while and haven't seen one another since I left for New York. Cal and I are planning a trip out to visit you before Christmas. We are flying up to Canada the first week in December to finalize the details for our vineyard wedding. We will be in Frisco the following week and would love to get together with you."

Felicia picked up her phone saw the message and replied. "Call me when you get a chance, so much to catch up on."

Within five minutes Candy called. "So, my best friend, how is life in San Fran?"

"Where do I start?" Felicia replied with excitement in her voice.

"Well, how about starting with Michael and you, how is that going?" Candy asked.

"For starters, Michael and his wife got divorced and he and I are now officially a couple, it's almost like we are married." She chuckled.

"I do hear from Michael when we have an article to work on and yes, he told me all about his divorce and how relieved he was to finally be able to have a whole relationship with you. I admire how you guys built your foundation as friends, a lot like Cal and I." Candy shared.

"Did he tell you about the wedding in England?" Felicia asked.

"He did and he also told me how it was a life altering experience seeing the children at the hospital. At one point, he said, he cried as he recalled that part of your trip. We all knew he was a very special person from day one. Cal told me the difference his presence made in your life." Candy went on.

"Candy." He said to me not long after he met him. "I believe this guy Michael was meant to be in Felicia's life. He reminds me somewhat of Adrian but there is an aura about him. Adrian was more business and success driven. Michael on the other hand is, I guess you could say, more laid back. He is driven to succeed in a different way, kind of with an energy source that you can just sense when you are around him. He is always smiling and just takes things in stride. I could see where Felicia could fall in love with him, his gentle nature and zest for a life beyond the material wealth Adrian worked so hard to attain."

Felicia began to tell the story. "And that is exactly what happened from the moment we met on the plane. I knew there was something special about him. I loved how at ease he was with himself, how polite and yes, he did look good but the other qualities he possessed were what really attracted me to him. What I love about him is how he energizes me. You know Candy, I turned most of my responsibilities at 21st First Century over to Jackie just so I could enjoy my time with Michael and what a time we are having."

Candy and Cal would be arriving in San Francisco three days before Thanksgiving.

"Why don't you guys celebrate Thanksgiving with us. It would be wonderful having you. Cal and Michael can do their thing one day, you and I can have a girl's night out and all of us can have a wonderful dinner together at our house. How does that sound?"

"Count us in, dear friend. And, did I hear you say "our" house?" Candy said lightly. "Yes, it is kind of is our house when he is here or I am at is place, he just makes me feel so at home no matter where we are."

"By the way, my parents want Michael and I to come to Vancouver for the Christmas holidays. They know all about Michael but have never met him in person." Felicia said.

"I am sure the McDonalds are going to embrace him like a son sweetie". Candice laughed. "And, I am sure in the near future, he will be just that."

"How did you know Michael and I are planning our wedding, I haven't spoken to you, did he tell you?" Felicia inquired.

"No, my friend, like I said earlier, you were destined to be with one another." Candy replied.

"Yes, we were, just like you and Cal and Jerry and Manning." Felicia said as they hung up.

Chapter 28

Emerald Eyes and Promises

Emerald Eyes and Promises

Thanksgiving with Candice and Cal went beautifully. One night the boys headed down to San Jose to meet up with some of Cal's friends. Cal had gotten two tickets to see a Sharks hockey game for he and Candy. She suggested he offer her ticket to Michael so she and Felicia could have a girl's night out while they attended the game. Cal was perfectly fine with that idea.

So, the guys headed out early Tuesday morning to visit Cal's friends and then on to the game. Felicia and Candice meanwhile had planned a day of shopping for a wedding dress and then some pamper time at the spa and hair salon. This was something Michael never really had in all his years with Melanie, a night out with the guys. He could see now why their relationship was so perfect. She respected his time alone to do his thing and he respected hers.

Michael and Felicia picked up all they needed for their dinner at Sasha and Kim's market on Wednesday night. The young turkey was seasoned and ready to go in the oven first thing in the morning. That was the beauty of this place, no frozen birds here, just a big, plump and juicy gobbler primed for cooking.

Our lovebirds were up at six. A fresh pot of coffee was put on for brewing as they began preparing a lavish celebration for their guests. Felicia was busy working on her three special dishes, mashed turnips, an asparagus dish using a mixture of cumin, coriander, turmeric, fresh grated ginger, lemon and orange juice and instead of the traditional holiday pie, Felicia sliced up fresh kiwi, mandarin oranges granny smith apples and topped the dish with yogurt covered raisins and slivered almonds.

Michael was put in charge of the stuffing which he would prepare using dried fruit and fresh cranberries. He would bake the mixture in a casserole dish to allow the juice from cranberries to soak into the seasoned bread cubes.

As he and Felicia worked side by side as they always loved doing in the kitchen, Michael went to the fridge and pulled out a chilled pitcher of Mimosa. As he poured the champagne and orange juice mix, Felicia came around behind him and put her arms around his stomach. "You just know how to celebrate life don't you my darling?"

Michael turned around to face Felicia and handed her a flute with the fresh mimosa. He wrapped his arm around hers bringing his glass to her lips as she did the same for him. "Quite the difference a year makes my love." He said as they took a sip of their drink. He took the glass along with his, set them down on the counter and began singing, "You will always be beautiful in my eyes."

Cal and Candice heard Michael singing as they approached the kitchen, took one another's hands and waltzed in.

"What a wonderful way to start this day with our dear friends." Cal said as he whirled Candy around the floor, past the center island where Michael had their drinks waiting. "To a lifetime of smiles." Michael cheered as the couples tapped their glasses.

As they sat in front of the fireplace enjoying the tray of sushi, Kim had prepared for them as a gift along with a delightful bottle of New Zealand Sauvignon Blanc from Sasha, Felicia's phone rang. She excused herself and went into the kitchen. "It's my mom honey, relax with Candy and Cal, I will be right back."

"Hi, sweetie, just calling to wish you and Michael a beautiful Thanksgiving. Dad and I took the ferry over to Victoria. Right now, we are sitting in The Library Room at The Empress Hotel having a cocktail until they call us for dinner."

"Mom, what a great way for you and Dad to spend your day. I love Victoria, boy, do I have so many fond memories growing up there." Felicia said.

Michael was engaged in conversation and never heard Felicia talking about Victoria.

"Honey, Mom wants to say hello."

'Be right there." Michael replied.

'Hi, Mrs. McDonald, Happy Thanksgiving." Michael said cheerfully.

"And Happy Thanksgiving Day to you Michael and by the way, thank you for the formality but you can call me Judy or better yet, why not Mom, it has a nice ring to it."

Michael looked over at Felicia. "Is it okay if I call her Mom?"

"Of course, my love, might as well get used to it." Felicia said with a smile.

"We will see you in a couple of weeks, looking forward to meeting you and your husband." Michael said before handing the phone to Felicia.

"How's Dad?" Felicia asked.

"He is right here, hold on. Ted, it's your baby girl." "Hi honey, we are looking forward to coming to California for Christmas. And, I can't wait to meet that special man in your life. From everything Mom has said about him, if he were to ask me for your hand in marriage, I may just have to say, yes." Her Dad chuckled.

"Dad, you are just too funny. You and Michael will get along great, he loves telling jokes, like you. I know you are going to love him, and I am certain he will take to you as well".

Felicia's mom got back on the phone. "See you in a few weeks sweetheart until then, love you, have a glorious celebration."

Michael and Felicia spent the next few weeks decorating the house and getting it ready for her parents visit.

Ted and Judy had booked a late afternoon flight into San Francisco in order to beat the holiday traffic and long lines going through customs.

As they awaited her parent's arrival, Felicia noticed Michael seemed to be a little nervous. "Honey, rest assured, you have nothing to worry about. My parents are really laid back and cool. You kind of remind me of my father in that you never seem to get too frazzled by anything." As she described her father, Michael seemed to feel more relaxed.

"Dad takes everything in stride. He and my mom met in high school. They grew up during the fifties, you know, that rock and roll era. I am sure my parents had their share of fun." Felicia said with a grin.

Michael was now calm.

"Oh, they were part of the doo-wop generation. I guess they would be, open- minded and kind of free spirited. I feel comfortable already."

As they exited customs, Felicia leaned into Michael and kissed him on the cheek. "Here they come honey, your future in-laws." Michael took one look at them, put his arm around Felicia and said. "Damn, your mom is as beautiful as you and your dad is quite a handsome man. They are a couple for the ages."

Judy McDonald was as glamourous as her daughter and, as fashionable too. Michael just couldn't get over how good of shape she and Ted were in. Both were dressed in jeans and leather jackets. Felicia's mom had her hair pulled back in a ponytail. She knew how to apply her makeup just like Felicia, using just the right colors and shades to compliment the eyes and lips. Her dad was in great shape. He had that outdoorsy, rugged look but clean shaven and neatly styled hair.

As Felicia was hugging her mom, Ted walked over to Michael, extended his hand and said. "So, you are the man our daughter raves about. I can see why."

Michael accepted his compliment and just smiled. "Welcome and Merry Christmas, Sir."

"You can call me Ted, then after you and my baby tie the knot, you can call me Dad." As he said that, he looked over at his daughter and winked.

Felicia led her mom over to Michael. "Honey meet my mom."

"And, you are as beautiful as your daughter told me." Michael said as he gave Judy a hug.

"And you Michael are so kind, thank you." Judy replied.

On the ride back to the house Ted sat up front with Michael and the two of them started telling one another jokes. Felicia leaned up behind Michael. "Didn't I tell you he was a jokester?"

After they arrived, unpacked, got changed and settled in, everyone gathered in the living room to celebrate Christmas Eve in front of the fire.

Felicia brought out a tray of croissants, fresh fruit and a pot of coffee while Michael put on a piano instrumental called, "Winter Solstice."

As Felicia and her mom curled up on the couch, Judy turned to her daughter and inquired. "Honey tell me all about this man you are so in love with."

Felicia looked at her mom with a sparkle in her eyes and began her story.

"It was like something out of a fairy tale. We met on the plane coming back from New Jersey and our friendship grew from there into what we share today. In the beginning Michael reminded me so much of Adrian but as I got to know him, I realized this man had many inner qualities. Adrian was always setting the bar higher and higher every time he achieved something, always wanting to be at the top of his game whereas Michael is so content taking life step by step and accepting things in their own time, like our relationship."

Felicia laid her head on her mom's lap and continued her story. "What I loved about Michael was how he never rushed himself into a relationship with me even though I was ready to have one with him. He let time take its course naturally, did what he had to in order to be, in a position to be able to give himself completely to me and me completely to him and that, is why our relationship is so solid. I can honestly say the he is the best friend I have ever had in my life and." Felicia paused. "The best lover."

Judy put her hand around her daughter's shoulders. "That is exactly how it was for your dad and me. We did grow up in a very free-spirited time when people were just letting it all hang out. Dad and I had some great times together. We loved going to concerts and partying as did everyone else but what separated us from the rest of the crowd was, we had goals and ambitions and never lost sight of them. While most of the people we knew burned out, your father and I made a good life for ourselves and because of that, you were able to have a good life."

"Mom, I was always so proud of both of you. Dad, being a history professor and you a psychologist. I was always being stimulated whenever we sat down at the dinner table. You and dad are so worldly. Growing up in that environment, I can see where my own ambitions and creativity came from not to mention, the ability as a woman to have achieved what I did in a man's world." Felicia looked up at her mom and squeezed her hand.

Ted and Michael had strolled over to look at the vinyl record collection. Michael was quite the music historian. At one point he had aspired to be a radio disc- jockey. Music was something that, was a constant in his life. He listened to all genres, not just rock. Jazz, classical and new age were all part of his extensive collection.

As Michael pulled out record after record and gave a little history lesson on the group's origins, style of music and any other anecdotes associated with an album, Ted just listened like he was a student in Michael's music history class.

Felicia and her mom looked over and saw how the two men were interacting. "Dad is truly enjoying his time with our future son-in-law. I don't think I have ever seen him so attentive, he usually is the one garnering the attention."

"Mom, Michael is no ordinary man, that is why I believe in him as a writer. He is well rounded and has a lifetime of stories to share, all will be enriching and beneficial to those who will read him one day."

Michael paused from his music history lesson for a moment, put down an album he'd been talking about and began to speak. "Ted, if I may, I am in love with your daughter. The love I am talking about has been built on a strong foundation through a bond of friendship, trust in one another and commitment to one another. We share so many things together yet respect and encourage one another's individuality." Ted was taking in every word as Michael proceeded.

"At this time, I would like to ask you for your daughter's hand in marriage with my word that the principles that brought us to this stage in our relationship will continue to grow our love into the future."

Ted reached out, took Michael's hand in his and looked him right in the eyes. "Michael, I know my daughter better than anyone except her mom and when I tell you I have never seen her this happy, I mean that from my heart." Both men now had tears in their eyes. Ted put his other hand over Michael's.

As Felicia and Judy looked from a distance, they saw the two men hug and embrace one another.

"You have my blessings Michael." Ted said as they turned to join their respective partners by the fire.

Michael had known a whole different kind of Christmas for the ten years he was with Melanie. It was always a big family affair with aunts, uncles, brothers and sisters, lot of kids running around and plenty of gifts being ripped open with piles of wrapping paper all over the floor. It was like reaching a crescendo, you spent three months preparing for this special time and in a few hours, it was all over.

The past two holiday seasons for him were different. It wasn't about gift giving, it was about giving thanks. It was about sharing from the heart, about reflection, intimate moments and joyous celebrations without all the pomp and circumstance. This was the way he and Felicia loved to embrace Christmas.

As the night approached the twelfth hour, that stroke before the midnight chimes rang in Christmas, Michael brought out a chilled bottle of champagne and poured for his guest, Felicia and himself. Raising his glass as he looked right at Felicia, he proposed a toast.

"To the women who will next year become my wife and to her Mom and Dad who will become my in-laws. Ted and Judy, I mean Mom, I give thanks and heartfelt blessings to you and your husband for your daughter and the wealth of happiness and love you instilled in her that she has chosen to share with me by accepting me into her life."

They all stood up, raised and tapped their flutes and embraced in a family hug.

Michael took Felicia's glass and set it on the table next to his. He looked over at the starburst clock on the wall. As the hands fell precisely upon the twelfth hour, he kneeled in front of Felicia, reached into his pocket, pulled out a box and opened it.

"My love, your father has given me his blessings for me to ask you to be my wife. I could think of no better scenario than here in front of the fireplace with your mom and dad present."

Michael took Felicia's hand in his and with the opened box in the other looked at her. "Will you spend all your days with me knowing I will continue to love, respect and honor you not only as a woman but as my wife?"

With tears streaming down her face she answered. "I have prayed for this day to come, yes Michael, I will spend all my days with you, continuing to love, respect and honor you not only as a man but as my husband."

The ring Michael eased onto Felicia's finger was one of a kind and held a sacred meaning. When he saw the ring, Jerry had given to Manning, Michael asked where he found such a beautiful and extraordinary keepsake. Jerry told him, he had it custom made through Catherine Cheshire, the owner of the antique shop Michael purchased the jade earrings from. Upon discovering that, he visited the shop and asked Catherine to have the same design but instead of the purple colored stone in the middle, Michael wanted a jade green emerald to match Felicia's eyes.

Felicia looked down at the ring, ran her fingers across it, and put it on display for her mom and dad. As she did, something magical seemed to transpire. The fire's light bounced off the emerald stone and lit up the color of Felicia's eyes, those emerald green eyes that Michael stared into the moment she sat next to him on the plane.

Chapter 29

Unwrapping the Surprise

Unwrapping the Surprise

Everyone had gone back home from the holidays. Spring would be here in just a few months. With Cal and Candice exchanging their vows at the end of April in the vineyards of the Okanagan Valley, Felicia and Michael decided, early Summer would be the best time for them to exchange theirs. They settled on the middle of July.

As much as they would have loved to have a double ring ceremony in the vineyards with Cal and Candy in the Spring or to wed along the beaches of the Oregon coast, they had come to an agreement, having their own ceremony would be best. Now, it was a matter of where their wedding would take place.

Felicia couldn't wait to get back to work and tell everyone about her engagement.

Michael was already conjuring up plans. He and Dana had talked about throwing an engagement party at the Plymouth Rock Inn once Michael proposed.

The atmosphere in the lobby of the Bristol Building had changed ever since Jerry retired. Felicia missed having him greet her with his accent and tip of the cap and her blowing him a kiss as she walked towards the elevator.

Life was no different at 21st Century. Although Felicia had turned most of her responsibilities over to Jackie, she still fostered the same family atmosphere just with her presence. When she arrived the Monday after the holidays, everyone was there to greet her. The first call of the day was gathering her staff to go over the agency's approach for the coming year. As she stood at the head of the long teak wood table placing her hands down as she always did, Jackie took notice of something glittering. "And how was your Christmas?" She asked slyly. "Anything special take place?"

Almost blushingly, Felicia looked over at Jackie smiled and said. "As a matter of fact, yes, my parents flew in from Vancouver to spend the holidays and meet Michael for the first time."

Jackie was one of the only ones besides Jerry and Cal who had known about Michael. All of them respected her privacy. For sure, many of the staff at the agency had an inclination something had changed in Felicia's life over a year ago but respected her privacy as well and just went about their daily business.

Today, all unfolded.

"For those of you who don't know, Michael and I met on the plane the morning I came back from landing the Adams Apparel account. Out of respect for one another, we decided to give our relationship time to grow, so we kind of kept our friendship at, pardon the pun, bay." Felicia paused. As she did, her staff seemed to be at the edge of their seats focusing on what was coming next.

"Christmas Eve at midnight and I mean right at the stroke of midnight, Michael proposed, and I accepted." Everyone at the table got up and gave Felicia a standing ovation with whistles and cheers filling the room. One by one her staff came over and hugged and congratulated her and of course asked to see the ring.

Jackie was the first one to give Felicia a hug and compliment her. "I have never seen such a beautiful ring in my life, so elegant and just, absolutely beautiful. I love how it sparkles and the stone matches your eyes so perfectly."

"Michael had it custom made and that was exactly what he told me he had in mind, to find a stone that would match the color of my eyes."

Felicia was beaming as she took her place at the head of the table and continued to address her staff. "I promise you will all meet him soon and," She said with a laugh. "You will all love him."

After the meeting adjourned, Felicia and Jackie walked back to her office. "Honey, I want to thank you for being such a trusted confidant, you know how hard it was for me to keep all of this under wraps for so long?" Jackie smiled. "Because of the love we have for you, all we wanted was to see you happy and we saw that. It wasn't a matter of who or what was changing you, it was that you had finally, been able to open up on a more emotional level than you had in years."

Jackie stood face to face with Felicia, took her hands into hers and said. "Please don't take this personally but, you were so ingrained in the agency and I know why, it was to keep yourself from falling apart. You never showed that side to any of us, all we saw was your strength. Now, we see a woman enjoying life to its fullest and my dear friend, it couldn't have happened to a more deserving person." Jackie said as she kissed Felicia on the cheek.

Over her intercom the receptionist informed Felicia she had an outside call coming in from, Michael. "I will talk to you later." Jackie said a she headed out to her own office.

"Hi honey." Michael voice was filled with happiness. "I just wanted to know if you will be coming in for lunch today, Dana let me come off the floor to prepare you a special dish."

"A special dish my love, I would be there to see you if you were serving me rolls and butter." Felicia chuckled.

"Well sweetie." Michael responded. "Do you think you can make it around three thirty, we will be closed getting ready for dinner. This way, I can give you my undivided attention."

"Don't you always sweetheart?" Felicia responded.

When she arrived, Dana was waiting at the front door to greet her and escort her in. As they entered the inn, something was different, the place was dark and empty. *"What the heck is going on."* She thought to herself.

Dana took Felicia by the hand and led her over to a special table in the far corner of the inn. The only light in the room was the candle flickering at the center of the table. The setting for two Dana had done, looked like something out of a magazine. As she sat Felicia down, she poured her and Felicia a glass of Napa Valley Chardonnay from her private collection. "To you and Michael, may your lives be filled with all you ever dreamed of."

Felicia tipped her glass to Dana's. 'So, Michael told you he proposed?"

"Yes, my dear, he called me into the office and, well you know what a sensitive man he is. Anyway, he told me how it all transpired with your mom and dad there, how elated he was and how perfect it all played out." Dana then asked to see the ring.

"As beautiful as he described it." She said holding it to the candlelight.

"I guess Michael is busy getting everything ready for the two of you. I will go and see if he needs any help." Dana hugged Felicia and walked back into the kitchen.

Within five minutes, the door to the kitchen opened. As Michael entered the room, Felicia looked over. As he approached the table, her jaw dropped. Instead of his usual, jeans and white dress shirt, Michael had on a black tuxedo. As he got closer to the table, she leaned back in her seat and tilted her head back. Michael stood alongside her, bent down and pressed his lips softly onto hers. Felicia sighed.

"My love, this night is for you." As he said that, he strolled over picked up a microphone and began to sing the song he had sung to her the night they had their first real kiss. As he got to the line, "The First Time Ever I kissed your mouth," he extended his hand to Felicia. She rose up from her seat and joined him.

Michael continued to sing. Felicia put her arms around his waist and stared into his eyes. As the song's last line was sung, she pulled him to her and said. "My darling husband to be, you know how to sweep me off my feet and that tux, you belong in GQ."

Michael led Felicia back to the table, eased her chair out and sat her down. "I will be back with the first dish."

As the doors swung closed behind him, the inn's lights came on with a soft glow.

Felicia took a sip of her wine and the doors opened. In Michael's hand was a small tray with a sterling silver platter. He walked over to the table, a white napkin draped over his arm and set the dish down next to the candle. Felicia looked down and saw not food but, a card that looked like an invitation.

She picked it up and began to read. As she did, the doors to the kitchen opened again.

"You are invited to celebrate Felicia and Michael's engagement."

One by one, the staff at the inn walked out of the kitchen carrying trays. They brought them over and set them up along the bar. As the last of the trays came out, the staff poured glasses of champagne and gathered around Felicia and Michael. A bottle and two full glasses were placed at the special couples table. Dana was the last to enter. She picked up the mic and began to speak.

"Tonight, we are here to celebrate the beginning of a lifetime of unity for two very special people." As the guests took their flutes of champagne and raised them, Dana continued. "To you Felicia and Michael, you are both blessings to all who know you and, you are loved by all whose lives you touch every day. Love and happiness to both of you forever, let the celebration begin."

Felicia looked at Michael. "Wow, I would never have known you had this planned."

"I have to give Dana all the credit for this, all I did was cook." Michael replied.

As they reveled in the jubilant atmosphere, singing, dancing, laughing and enjoying dish after dish of delicacies, Felicia put her lips up to Michael's ear. "Now, that our relationship has been sanctioned, I would love to have you finally come up to my office and meet everyone at the agency."

"I was waiting for the invite sweetheart, can't wait." Michael said accepting Felicia's offer.

Chapter 30

101 Hearts

101 Hearts

Jackie was planning her own little surprise. After Felicia made the announcement about the engagement and remarked that staff would finally be meeting Michael, Jackie went into motion.

Her boss hadn't stayed late at the office for quite some time so figuring out a way to get her to come back once she left was the challenge. "*I'll figure it out.*" Jackie said to herself. As she pondered that scenario, something just struck her. "*Valentine's Day, that's it. I will see if I can.*" She paused the thought as her phone rang.

"Hi Jackie, it's Michael." Jackie met Michael a few months after he started working at the inn. Felicia and she would come in for lunch to get away from the agency. It was a great place to have informal business meetings.

Michael had waited on the two of them since day one and became an extended friend with her through Felicia.

"You know." Michael started out. "I have never been to the office to meet Felicia's coworkers. She mentioned to me at our little engagement party at the inn about coming in to meet everyone. I thought with Valentine's Day coming up, instead of her and I going out to dinner, having you and the other people at the agency get together somewhere." Felicia listened as Michael continued.

"My place is within walking distance to the office, what would you think about having a party here?" Michael asked. "I mean, I will leave you in charge of organizing it, I am just offering my studio. It is big enough to accommodate everyone and like I said, close to the office."

Michael, are you a mind reader or something?" Jackie laughed. "I was just thinking how I could pull off having an engagement party for the two of you and you come to the rescue."

"I just figured it was a great way to meet everyone in a festive atmosphere." Michael noted. "I am sure Felicia doesn't get many chances to mingle with all of you outside of the office. For me, it takes the edge off. I can call our friends over in Sausalito and have them cater, would it be okay to invite them as well?"

"Michael, I know exactly who you are referring to, Sasha and Kim, right?"

'You know them?" Michael asked.

"Yes, Felicia turned me on to them years ago when I needed some catering done. I have been going to the market ever since. It is a little drive from where I live so I usually do my shopping there on Saturday mornings. Because, it is just my boyfriend and I and neither one of us are maestros in the kitchen, they will put together a weekly meal plan. All we do is pick it up and follow the recipes."

"They are quite remarkable when it comes to running their business the right way." Michael boasted about the gourmet market.

Time was flying by ever since Michael and Felica returned from England. With Valentine's Day a little over a week away, Michael would take care of the catering.

What a blessing how everything was panning out perfectly. The day of love fell on a Saturday and it was the weekend he and Felicia would be in Sausalito. He told Jackie she and her boyfriend could spend the weekend at his place. This way they could decorate and do what they needed for the party as well as being there to welcome all the guest. Michael would tell Felicia he had something special for her at his place and that is how Jackie would be able to pull this whole celebration off.

"See my dear, sometimes life just has a way of falling perfectly into place." Michael said to Jackie as he hung up the phone.

February 13th, this was going to be a lucky day. Contrary to what some people want to plant in their heads regarding superstitions and Michael was not one of them, tonight would be a prelude to the grand celebration happening at his place tomorrow night.

Instead of ordering take out which they liked to do on Friday nights, Michael and Felicia were going to pick up fresh dough and yes, Kim and Sasha carried that as well knowing many of their customers liked to create their own pizza at home instead of having it delivered. Create, is what Felicia and Michael do when they get in the kitchen and as they both found out through experimenting, there isn't much you can't put on a pizza. Each of them would have their own dough to work with.

Michael choose artichoke hearts, granny smith apples, feta cheese, spinach and celery as his toppings. Felicia went in a different direction with hers; chopped up clams and fresh garlic layered in Italian pecorino cheese, a sprinkling of olive oil, fresh ground oregano topped with basil leaves. They would then compliment the pizzas with beer instead of wine. A New England style hoppy IPA for Michael's and a German Pilsner for Felicia's.

As tough as it was for Michael to keep tomorrow's surprise inside, the pizza and beer did wonders keeping him distracted.

Even tougher was hiding the ultimate surprise he would unveil to her at the party.

Sasha and Kim arrived at four-thirty and began setting up the food.

The guests began arriving at five as requested to give them a chance to settle in before the six o'clock arrival of the celebrants.

In total there were twenty-two guests. Jackie and her boyfriend, Sasha and Kim, and the staff of eighteen which in comparison to the huge payrolls other advertising firms employed, spoke volumes about Felicia's ability to maximize her staff by hiring the right people. There were no specialists just a small dedicated group of extremely talented artists with excellent business and marketing savvy. This was how the family at the agency was able to rise above its competitors and be the cream of the crop when it came to consumer appeal.

As the six o'clock hour arrived, there was a turning of the lock on the front door. As Felicia entered the studio, Michael stood in the doorway to watch her reaction. "Oh Lord, someone's been keeping a secret." Felicia said as she panned the room. "Michael, how did you keep all of this inside?" She turned around and jumped into his arms. "Honey, this was Jackie's idea, I just provided the space."

Felicia ran over to Jackie and spun her around. "You are the best, the absolute best."

As everyone celebrated their engagement Michael kept looking over to the far wall making sure Felicia hadn't noticed anything different or out of place in the studio. He was certain to move the tall rubber plant in front of the wall and prayed Felica wouldn't notice it had been relocated from its usual resting place.

What a great time everyone was having. Michael had saved the best for last.

As the party was winding down, he took out a blindfold and placed it over Felicia's eyes. "Honey, I have another surprise for you." He walked her over and stood her facing the wall in front of the plant. As he slowly pulled the planter away, an easel stood with a white sheet draped over what appeared to be, a large painting. Michael pulled the blindfold away from Felicia's eyes but told her to keep them closed as he walked over to the wall and took hold of the sheet.

"Okay, darling, you can open your eyes now." As she did Michael tugged at the sheet, pulling it away from the canvas and letting it drop onto the floor. "For you my love, Happy Valentine's Day."

Felicia stood there, tears forming in her eyes as she stared at the piece of art.

"It is titled, 101 Hearts." Michael pointed out.

Michael wiped the tears from her eyes and said. "After I finished, I counted the number of hearts and lo and behold, there were one hundred and one, just like the movie with the dalmatians."

Varying hues of pinks and reds covered the back of the canvas while white abstract hearts in all sizes made up the forefront. In the center was the largest heart with smaller ones reaching out to the sides and top. At the bottom it was signed, Michael Langston.

"I always knew you aspired to write a book. Michael, did you know that you are also an incredible painter. I am lost for words honey except to say, it takes my breath away."

After all the guests had departed, Michael and Felicia thanked Kim and Sasha for the incredible food they prepared and Jackie and her boyfriend, Carlo for decorating and organizing the party.

As she stood in front of the easel admiring the four foot by six-foot painting, Felicia wondered where it would best be hung. She wanted to showcase Michael's talent and envisioned it hanging on a wall by itself where others could appreciate it as well.

Michael was helping Jackie put away the glasses in the kitchen when Felicia came in. "Honey, what would you think if I were to hang it on the wall outside my office. It is big enough and the painting would really stand out."

Michael answered. "Let's bring the painting with us and stop by your office tomorrow to see where it would be best to hang it."

"You're okay with that Michael, I mean if we hang it at 21st Century?" Felicia inquired.

"As long as you promise it will hang on the wall of our own home someday." Michael replied.

"Our own home one day honey, you mean someplace besides, Sausalito?" Felicia asked.

Michael sounded so confident as he spoke. "I can see us northwest of the border in a smaller home, on a lake one day." He put his arms across Felicia's shoulders and said. "I already have the picture, perfect house design in mind. Once I get that advance for my first book, we will build it."

Felicia looked right into Michael's eyes and knew he was serious.

Chapter 31

The Connection

The Connection

They arrived at the office early Sunday morning. Felicia had on her stretch pants and a white button down, halter that wrapped around her waist. The outlines of her breasts were accented by the tight tee. Michael had on white yoga drawstring linen pants and a black muscle shirt.

Felicia unlocked the door to 21st Century and peeked in. Sometimes, one or two of her staff would come in to tackle a deadline but the office was silent. As they walked past the reception area Michael's eyes were panning the floor, taking everything in. He was like a kid in a candy store. He had never set foot inside the agency and found himself in awe of just how ultra-modern and expansive it was.

The walls in the agency were painted in a light lilac color which accented the white contemporary furnishings. New Age music was piping through the sound system filling the room with a sense of calm and relaxation. The eastern philosophies Michael and Felicia believed in were evident in the agency's total design from the color scheme to the sleek-lined chairs and tables.

As Michael glanced about the room, he was amazed at the number of awards the agency had received.

There were no cubicles like one would see on the floor of most offices. Felicia did not believe in closing her staff in to three by three cubbies, she felt it would hinder a person's creativity. The open floor plan allowed for interaction without having to look over a wall or enter an enclosed space. Felicia led Michael towards her office.

Her office was for the most part open with a clear transparent front and a glass door supported at each end by two floor-to-ceiling walls, Michael guessed this was where Felicia was talking about hanging the painting. He placed the painting against the clear glass.

At the base of each wall was a table adorned with two soft white leather chairs where, perspective clients would sit awaiting their meeting with Felicia, not in some stuffy reception area.

The tables had marketing and advertising periodicals neatly arranged in a semicircle. In the center of the arrangement was a magazine with Felicia's face on the cover. It was a copy of, "Women Leaders in Business."

Michael looked at Felicia and said. "I would love to read that honey. That picture of you on the cover in your white blouse, the sensual music in here and, overall atmosphere in this office is very stimulating." He pulled Felicia to him and the two shared a very long and passionate kiss.

There were never any inhibitions with Felicia since the first night they shared intimacy when it came to making love to Michael. She was enamored by his gentleness and was always eager to let herself go completely. She welcomed any opportunity to share new experiences with him.

As they kissed, she pushed her fingers through his belt loops and led him into her office. Laying down on top of her desk, she pulled Michael on top of her. Michael nestled himself against the skin-tight material in between her legs as Felicia pulled up her shirt to expose her bare breasts. As they felt themselves getting more and more turned on, Felicia could feel the wetness pushing through the spandex material. She felt total abandonment, pushed Michael's thighs back from her and rolled over on her stomach.

As she dropped her legs to the floor Michael pulled down her tights. As Felicia slowly pushed her backside into him Michael leaned forward and gently cupped her breasts. As she slid back and forth Michael went with her every movement knowing she would direct him to her pleasure spot.

Lovemaking for them was always slow and gentle consisting of long sessions of foreplay. They enjoyed the erotic feeling they felt from soft touching and passionate kissing sessions before making love.

The sensuousness of them being in a public place, somewhat a little risky if one of her staff decided to come into the office at that moment was a complete turn on for them.

The climax they experienced was so intense, Felicia laid her face down, gently biting her lips. As she pushed herself deep into Michael thighs, she took her outstretched arms and grabbed the edge of her desk while letting out a soft moan. Michael stood upright as Felicia rocked and quivered against him. He grabbed her by her waist and gave one final thrust before collapsing against her bare back. The two of them slithered off the desk and lay in a heap on the floor.

In the heat of it all, knowing they could've been caught, they both lay there drenched and naked, looked at one another and burst out laughing.

Felicia had a closet in her office with several changes of clothes. She slipped into another pair of spandex pants and slipped on Michael's favorite, a white, laced up Bohemian style blouse. She tossed Michael a pair of sweats and one of her seventies tie-dyed tee shirts. She put their soaked clothes into a duffle bag.

As she was brushing her hair and freshening up her makeup, Michael picked up the magazine with Felicia on the cover and began to read the article. As he read further into the story, Michael smiled. He knew he had a very extraordinary women in his life. He also knew that they had a divine connection which he had felt all along. And, there it was on page 73.

Wind swept sea,
Sand castles and memories.
So much I have seen thorough theses pale blue skies,
I often wonder, if only, I could fly.
Far away lies the end, a still, quiet mystery,
Horizons begin there where my eyes meet the sea.
A grain of sand where once stood a sand castle,
It's all in the wind now, it's all in the wind now.
Written by: The Poetry Man

Michael read the explanation Felicia had given the interviewer about the writing. "When I look at the poem, it reminds me of growing up on Vancouver Island. I would spend my days on the beach watching the seagulls fly over the ocean. I always dreamed of being able to fly. There I was looking at the gulls in flight thinking, "If only I had your wings." Ironic, I would find that poem.

I often wondered who really wrote it and why they didn't put their real name on it.

Felicia exited her office and saw Michael reading the article. She glanced down to see what page he was on. "Honey come back into my office, I want to show you something. She extended her hand as Michael closed the magazine and put it back into the center of the table.

She walked him over to the very same poem Michael was reading in the article. As he stood in front of the framed writing Michael never said a word.

Upon reading the article and with Felicia showing him the poem on her office wall, Michael knew the connection had to be the small bookshop in Victoria.

Chapter 32

Manning Osborne of Kingstanding

Manning Osborne of Kingstanding

Michael dropped Felicia off at her office around ten on Monday. He parked the Rover in the underground garage and walked over to Fisherman's Wharf.

Dana had given him the day off from the inn.

As he sat at his favorite café, sipping cappuccino he looked across the bay to the cliffs of Sausalito and began to recollect all the amazing events and people that had come into his life since that rainy morning he met Felicia on the plane.

There was Cal and Candice, Jerry and Manning, Dana, Catherine, Ted and Judy McDonald, Jackie and Carlo, Sasha and Kim, and most importantly, the woman who would soon be his wife.

He thought about the wedding in England, the off the road motel in Lincoln City, Oregon, McCovey's Cove, the Christmas Eve proposal and the two engagement parties, the heart painting that was now hanging on the wall at 21st Century Advertising, and the first time he and Felicia shared their passion for one another.

As he reached into his backpack to get his phone, his hands ran across the embossed letters of the journal Manning had gifted him the night before they left England to return to San Francisco. He recalled the words Jerry said when he handed it to him. *"Perhaps when you sit down to write your book, this journal will find its way as one of those publications."*

Michael's mind was racing as he lifted the journal out from his backpack. He placed it on his lap, ran his hand over the cover and opened the first of the pages. As he read into the stories, Michael became more and more mesmerized by Manning's life and thought to himself. *"Jerry was right, this is definitely something I can put into a book."*

In between stories, Michael would pause to absorb what he had just read, take a sip of coffee and find himself thinking about how, Vancouver Island would be the perfect place for he and Felicia to be wed.

As the foghorn from the tug passing under the bridge went off, Michael closed the journal and placed it back in his bag and pulled out his phone. He had become so absorbed in the journal that he lost track of time.

Felicia had sent him a message that read: *"Know you are off today honey, enjoy. Just wanted to know if you want to meet at your favorite cappuccino place for a bite to eat?"*

It was already close to noon. *"Funny you mention the café, I am sitting here as I write this to you. See you when you get here sweetie, something to share."* Michael texted back.

The temperature was creeping up from the cool thirty-eight it was two hours ago to a comfortable fifty-three degrees when Felicia arrived. Michael got up gave her a warm hug and kiss.

They both ordered the house special salad. Hearts of romaine lettuce, shredded carrots, chopped up spinach, avocado and alfalfa sprouts with a melon flavored creamy dressing. While they waited for their food to arrive, Felicia announced she and Jackie had to go to Sacramento on Friday to meet with a new client and asked if he wanted to join her on the trip.

Michael thought about it for a minute.

"Would you mind if I just hung out at my place while you are away? I have an article to get done for Candice and thought I could use this weekend to work on it."

"Not at all. You haven't had much time to chill lately with everything going on. I was going to drive home after the meeting, but it might be nice for Jackie and I to have a girl's weekend away as well."

Michael just smiled back at Felicia. "Everything always works out so perfect for us."

Felicia spent Thursday night with Michael at the studio. She was meeting Jackie at the office the next morning at eight thirty. San Francisco was more of a direct route to Sacramento than Sausalito, so it made sense for her to stay in the city and it gave her and Michael a chance to spend some romantic time together before they went their separate ways for the weekend.

By Friday evening, Michael had completed Manning's journal. As he sifted through the pages, he was jotting down notes in his own journal to see how he could intertwine Manning's incredible life into at least, a short story. The more he looked over his notes, he became confident he could put enough of a storyline together to write a novella.

Michael was very adept at taking a situation and creating not only a lively descriptive of what took place, he could paint very real and colorful characters. The many years of writing poetry enabled him to create the kind of visual imagery that takes the reader into the story. This was exactly the way Manning's journal read and this was why he knew it would make for a remarkable story and perhaps even, a screenplay. *"This is going to be my first book."* He thought to himself as he began penning, "Manning Osborne of Kingstanding."

And what a weekend it turned out to be for, "The Poetry Man."

Felicia said if he wanted to call, she would love to hear from him but, she also knew how important this alone time was for him. She said as she was leaving Friday morning. "Honey, you once told me, when your creative juices get flowing, you get totally absorbed in whatever it is you are creating so don't feel bad if you pull yourself away for the next couple of days. I will pick you up Sunday after I drop Felicia off and we can spend the evening catching up." Michael did call her right before retiring to bed on Friday and Saturday to wish her sweet dreams and give her a kiss goodnight.

Contrary to crawling into bed, Michael was filled with an inexhaustible energy and was up writing the entire time Felicia was away. The words just flowed.

As he wrote, he envisioned a future hall-of-fame running back, breaking through the line and bursting, eighty-five yards at full speed along the sidelines, crossing the goal line and pumping his fist against his chest while raising his other hand to the heavens to thank God for the gift he was given.

By Sunday afternoon, he had an entire novella drafted for editing, to get it print ready. One hundred and eight pages and thirty thousand plus words later, Michael was holding in his hands, the pages of his first book ever.

As he came to the last sentence, he felt a huge emotional rush take over and burst into tears. "I did it!" He exclaimed as he jumped up from his computer and pumped his fist against his chest while saluting the heavens with the other saying out loud, "Thank you God for this gift!"

He was so elated over the accomplishment, he almost missed Felicia's call. It was now, one thirty.

"Well, hello my handsome man. We just left Sacramento and are headed back. We should be back by three thirty or so. I will drop Jackie off and come by to get you if that is okay." Felicia sounded excited.

"Can't wait to see you darling. It has been quite the weekend, far more accomplished than I could have ever anticipated." Michael sounded excited as well.

"I can't wait to hear all about it and to tell you about the fun Jackie and I had. See you soon, love you." As she hung up the phone, she glanced into her mirror at the wrapped package sitting on the back seat.

"Michael is going to love it." Jackie said.

Instead of waiting for Felicia to show up at his place, Michael packed his overnight bag, tucked the manila folder with the story in it, showered and put on Felicia's favorite outfit along with the scent she loved. He had about twenty-five minutes before Felicia and Jackie would get to the office, enough time to pick up a dozen roses for his beloved.

As Felicia pulled up to the curb to let Jackie out, Michael walked over, opened her door, all the while holding the bouquet behind his back, and extended his hand to help her on to the sidewalk.

As she stood up, Michael pulled the roses out and placed them in Felicia's hand. She took one look at them and said. "Baby, I have never seen such beautiful colored roses."

"They are known as Ebb Tides The deep purple color is very rare. I have never seen anything like it either. Like you honey, rare and stunningly beautiful." Michael walked her around to the passenger side and opened the door. As she slid in to the seat, Michael reached over and buckled her in. Their lips met. "Welcome home love, I missed you." He eased her door closed.

"Quick stop at the market to pick up our dinner." Michael said. "I called Kim earlier and asked if they could put something together for us."

When they got there the women were waiting curbside with a picnic basket. "Breakfast in bed, as you requested Michael." They giggled as Sasha handed Michael the basket.

Chapter 33

Novella

Novella

After they soaked in the tub, Michael laid a blanket out on the bed and arranged the dishes on a large folding tray. Their dinner consisted of two fresh sourdough rolls garnished with olive oil and roasted peppers topped with mozzarella cheese squares, fresh melon and steak tartare and a bottle of French Beaujolais, a special gift from Dana for the engagement party.

"Are you ready for your first surprise honey?" Felicia called out as she slowly opened the glass door to reveal herself. Michael turned around as Felicia walked towards him in a gold sequined mesh baby doll. Her eyes and lips were accented with a gold metallic eye shadow and glimmering lip gloss.

"Totally tantalizing." Michael said as they shared a soft, just barely touching lips, kiss. "Don't want to mess up those lips gorgeous lips." He whispered as he tasted the flavor of her mouth.

"Not to worry honey, there's enough to last and last." Felica cooed.

Next to the bed was the wrapped box Felicia brought back from Sacramento. She handed it to Michael as he poured the wine and said. "I found this in a little thrift store in Sacramento and thought of you."

Michael pulled off the bow and gold wrapping and eased the lid off the box. As he looked inside, he couldn't believe Felicia found this. As he lifted the winged seagull sculpture out of the box, he studied the beautiful piece of burlwood it was mounted on. On the back was a small metal plaque that had the name John Perry on it.

"This is from the seventies. The artist I believe is from Oregon. I have always admired how graceful and delicate he made them and the choice of wood for mounting." As he continued gazing at the sculpture Michael remarked. "Another piece of nature's art for our home."

He placed it down on the bed next to the tray. "Now, I have something for you." Michael pulled out the manila folder and handed it to Felicia. She opened it and read the title.

"Michael, do you know what this is, this is your first book. She said as tears rolled down her cheeks. "You wrote this while I was away?" Felicia stared at the title in disbelief. "You actually wrote over one hundred pages in two days."

"I wanted to surprise you and get it printed in book form, but I wanted you to be the first to see it. My plan tonight was to begin reading it to you."

"I am still somewhat shocked you could accomplish this in two days, you didn't get much sleep, did you?"

"No, honey. I tried but after we said goodnight on the phone, the words just kept coming and I wrote and wrote and wrote. It was all streaming through me like that voice I heard years ago. As I finished it, I cried. It was like someone had taken over my thought process, took my hands and just kept me typing until the very last word."

"How about if I massage you while you read?"

"That was my other surprise." Felicia said as she took out a bottle of oil, took off the cap and held it up to Michael's nose to smell.

"Eucalyptus, a very soothing scent". He said as he dabbed a drop on to Felicia's finger.

After they finished the divine meal Kim and Sasha had prepared for them, Michael cleared the tray off the bed. He sat with his back facing her. As

Felicia poured a dripping of oil on him and rubbed it into his skin, he began reading the story.

Felicia and Michael planned it so they could stay home on Monday which worked out well since they were up all night. After his massage, Michael propped his head up on a pillow and continued to read as Felicia rested her head on his chest.

"Though we were just twelve then, I have never forgotten how we felt for one another. When we were forced to go our own ways, I knew I would have to find a way to carry on. The years have come and gone and everything you see is, a reflection of what my heart has felt all those years. I never knew when you would be in my life forever, but I did know that day would come."

Michael took a break from reading and put the folder down. He had gone through eighty-five pages. "Honey, I would love for you to finish up the last chapter if you are not too tired."

"I am wide awake and loving every word, what an emotional love story. How Jerry and Manning never stopped loving one another after all those years and to think, we were at their wedding."

Felicia went on. "You said you need to edit it before printing right? Would you let me do that for you?"

"I would love you to, you know the characters as well as I do, and it would be an honor to have my partner be my editor." Michael replied.

Felicia fell in love with the story from the very first page.

She knew the book would attract a huge following, something inside told her so. She also saw a screenplay being made from this story, it was just a matter of getting it into the right hands and Felicia knew exactly the right people whose hands to put it in.

"Michael, I would love to be your PR person on this." Felicia said.

"You are hired." Michael said as they kissed each other good night.

Chapter 34

Vineyard Wedding

Vineyard Wedding

Felicia got busy working on Michael's book. She was a whiz at editing and had it finished in just three days. The only thing missing now, was the front cover.

She texted Michael. *"Honey, please call me after you finish up at the inn."*

Michael responded back. *"Will do better than that, how about if I come by the office and look at that beautiful painting outside your office you told me about. Lol."*

"Lol, wonderful, it's a date, see you around three." Felicia texted back.

Michael arrived around three fifteen. "Well, hello Mr. Langston." Felicia's receptionist, Ingrid Olson said with a smile as Michael walked in the door. "I had a great time Saturday. Thank you for welcoming all of us into your home, it really is a place to die for the way you have it decorated, all artsy and comfy. Not too many men have that kind of decorating flair. Kudos to you, Mr. Langston."

Ingrid was twenty-six years old. She had immigrated to California from Sweden. Her blonde hair and blue eyes were as stunning as she was at almost six two in her heels. "Felicia is expecting you, I can walk you back this way you can see how she designed the office. It really looks like something out of a magazine." She said so proudly. "Oh and, wait till you see what's hanging on the wall outside her office."

As Ingrid led the way, Michael said nothing, he just smiled to himself thinking about what transpired in that very office a few days before. As they approached Felicia's working area, she was already outside, standing next to the painting Michael presented to her at the engagement party.

"Perfect place for it honey." Michael said as he winked at her.

Ingrid handed her a box and headed back to her desk.

"Let's go into my office sweetheart, I have something for you." Michael took a seat in the overstuffed chair. Felicia leaned up against her desk and handed Michael the file folder box. "Open it honey."

Inside was a bound manuscript.

"Manning Osborne of Kingstanding." Now, that has a nice ring to it. Michael said as he leafed through the pages.

"It's, all there, edited and formatted in a standard book size. All you need now is a cover design and you have your first ready to publish book." Felicia was excited.

"Love, I can't believe you did all this so quickly." Michael commented.

"You wrote it in two days, now that's, an unbelievable accomplishment and testament to your gift as a writer." Felicia responded.

Felicia put her hands-on Michael's face and looked into his eyes. "You are the author and I am your agent and together we make one hell of a team."

Felicia stood up, walked around her desk, pulled up her chair and sat down facing Michael as if she were talking to a client and presenting a proposal.

"As I was editing your book, something hit me." Michael leaned forward in his chair as Felicia went on. "What if you and I opened up our own publishing company and not only published your books but opened the door to other aspiring writers like you."

"Go on, hon, I like the sound of this." Michael said encouragingly.

"Remember we talked about doing missionary work and giving something back? With our own company, we can do that because all the proceeds from your books will stay in house." Felicia continued.

You are a very gifted writer able to capture a scene so vividly with words. Imagine the kind of book you can write based on our work with children in other countries. Better yet, imagine setting up an endowment fund for those children to provide them with food, shelter, medical needs and an education."

"*Shelter.*" Michael repeated to himself. "Better known around the world as, 'Lillian Pines.'"

"I know we can do it Michael. I have an expansive network of contacts who would love to be a part of a pay it forward project like this."

As Felicia was talking, Michael was already painting mental pictures for the cover of his first book. It would depict where Manning and Jerry resided.

He envisioned a rolling meadow with lavender fields as a backdrop and wooden shingled, small paned windowed, stone row houses along a cobblestone street. The scene would center in on Manning's house with its chimney and a billow of smoke rising into a clear blue sky. On the front of the house vines of climbing English Ivy would frame the windows and accent the stone facing. The cobblestone street would wind its way past the houses and up to the fields.

As he shared his vision with Felicia, she was already thinking of an artist at 21st Century that could capture this perfectly. She dialed her extension. "Amanda dear, would you mind coming to my office, I have a very interesting project that I want to discuss with you. Please bring your sketch pad."

Amanda Turner walked over and gave Michael a hug. "I have to say, the party at your place was one of the best I have ever gone to."

She was very Bohemian in her style and quite the looker for a woman in her sixties. Her fashion was atypical for an artist living in SoHo during the Pop art explosion. She had cropped, shoulder length, black hair tucked behind her ears. She wore a tan cashmere beret with a matching sweater, a floor length paisley skirt and tan suede ankle boots. Her choice of makeup would always accent her wardrobe. Today, it was flesh colored tones on her eyes and lips and a pale pastel orange on her eyelids and the same shade lip liner to finish off her stunning look.

Amanda spent her early career after graduating from Parsons in fashion design. She and Michael talked about her studio in SoHo and how his place brought back so many memories.

She began her story.

"Greenwich Village was where it was all happening not only in music but art as well. I was blessed to be around so many talented and gifted artists. The established ones were supportive of the up and coming ones. I was fortunate to be able to go to a great art school, but my real education came from hanging out with all those talented people."

She shared more with Michael. "I got my start designing clothes and jewelry but, I wanted to make a statement that was more verbal than physical and that is what brought me to San Francisco. It was a struggle. I was homeless at one point, selling my jewelry was enough to feed me not enough, to provide shelter."

Amanda gestured over to Felicia and said. "She rescued me and gave me a new start not only in my career but in life." A tear fell from her as she recalled walking into her job the first day. "From the offset, I was made to feel an integral part of this amazing and creative family. At sixty-four, I was wondering like the song says, *"Will you still need me, will you still feed me."*

Michael began explaining his idea for the cover of his book. As he went through each scene he'd envisioned, Amanda was busy sketching and capturing what he was saying. *"And, the cobblestone street would wind out past the houses and up to the fields."*

She put her pencil down and held up her pad to show what she had drawn. Felicia and Michael looked at the picture and then at one another.

"There's the cover of your first book, my love." Felicia said as she got up and hugged Amanda.

It was now after five which was later than usual for Felicia to be at the office. Michael suggested they head back over to The Plymouth Rock Inn, for dinner, some cocktails and then spend the night at the studio.

Felicia accepted the invitation and off they went.

As they awaited dinner, Michael proposed a toast. "To my agent, best friend and fiancé, will you accompany me on a trip to a very special place after Cal and Candy's wedding?" Felicia laughed. "But we are going to a very special place, the vineyards."

"I know honey, but I had somewhere else in mind after that. Let's fly down to Seattle and rent a car. We could drive up the coast to Port Angeles and take the ferry over to Victoria." He went on. "We haven't decided where we will hold our wedding and for some reason that area of Vancouver Island may be our calling. We could go and just check it out. What do you think honey, you in?"

"You bet I am sweetheart." Felicia said as she raised her glass back to him.

The vineyard was as picturesque as any place to exchange vows. For Cal and Candice, it was everything they wanted, a simple, outdoor setting with a family style atmosphere. Twenty people including the bride and groom were in attendance. After their vows were exchanged, everyone sat down at a long table to dine on a five-course meal. All the dishes were prepared at the main house by the vineyard's owner, Luis Rosario and his wife Gabriela, whom Candice had become friends with during her photo shoots.

She was a guest of honor every time she arrived. Today, the bride and groom and their family and friends would be treated to the finest in Portuguese cooking and of course, the finest of the vineyard's wines.

Michael felt right at home having written articles about the Okanagan Valley vineyards. Candice had a staff photographer flown in to take pictures. Conde' Nast wanted to do a feature on the wedding and wanted Michael to write the article.

Candice was dressed in a white, long sleeved laced dress with a V-necked laced insert and flowing train. Cal was in all white as well. His size was well suited. As he stood next to Candice, the sun was directly overhead. The rays formed a haloed light frame around them, something the photographer was captured impeccably.

Chapter 35

Weekend in Victoria

Weekend in Victoria

The ride up Washington's northwest corridor into Port Angels was breathtaking. The Sequim Valley, known for its lavender fields would not be in full bloom until the first week in July.

Michael took Felicia's hand in his. "Just think honey, if we do have our wedding on the Island, we could drive back though here and attend the lavender festival. I was up this way when they were in bloom and what a magnificent site it was, a carpet of bright purple flowers running for miles and miles along the drive."

For the last week in April, it was still a little cool. Temperatures fluctuated in the low to mid-fifties, chilly enough for Michael and Felicia to don their goose down jackets. The drive from Seattle to the Port Angeles terminal had taken a little over two hours.

It was just past eleven when they parked and secured their auto and passenger tickets.

Walking back towards the car Michael looked across the street and pointed. "The ferry begins loading at 12:20, gives us enough time to have breakfast. There's a diner, right across the street, we can watch the ferry dock from our seats."

After the ferry docked, they paid the check and headed back to the car.

The cars began pulling onto the deck. "Wow, Michael, it holds quite a bit doesn't it?" Felicia was amazed.

"This ferry holds over one hundred cars and a thousand passengers, I looked it up the first time I made the trip." Michael explained.

The ride into Victoria's Inner Harbor would take close to two hours.

Michael and Felicia grabbed a cup of coffee and headed out to the bow of the ship. With the wind blowing through their hair, they both held their heads back, breathed in deep and let the fresh ocean air envelop them.

As the ferry made her way into the capitol city of British Columbia, Felicia grabbed Michael and gave him a big kiss. "I love you darling."

Felicia pointed to the house boats lining the sea wall to the entrance of the harbor. "Maybe, we could live in one of those." She said as she hugged him closer. The ferry navigated its way into the docking area and within minutes the cars and passengers were offloading.

"There she is." Michael gestured. "The Empress."

They had secured a penthouse apartment in the middle of the city through a friend of Felicia's parents. Frederick Gardner was a professor at the University of Victoria and a lifelong friend. He resided in Oak Bay and had begun investing in city real estate before the boom took place. What was once a quaint city was now a sprawling metropolis. By converting his four condos into timeshares, his attorney advised him, it would be more profitable and less maintenance for the retired teacher.

The suite was located on the top floor of an eighteen-story high rise. As Michael unlocked the door, he placed their one suitcase on the ground by the entranceway. He and Felicia headed to the wrap around deck and opened the sliding glass doors. As they panned the view of the harbor, the Parliament Buildings and Empress Hotel, Michael began to feel something spiritual filtering through him. It was kind of like the feeling he would get every time he wrote but this was a little different. He turned Felicia to him and looked into those beautiful emerald green eyes. They always made him melt. As he looked at her, he recalled thinking on several occasions the sense of connection he felt with her.

It was like a magnet had drawn them together on the plane and now the city of Victoria was acting as that magnet.

Included with their condo were two bicycles which were parked in the second bedroom. "Let's explore the city." Michael said as he wheeled the bikes out.

They headed out the garage towards Government Street.

To the left was the Empress, to the right stood Inner Harbor with its *"Welcome to Victoria"* sign on the grassy knoll, made with flowers, the Provincial Museum and The Parliament Buildings.

As they drove past the museum, Michael stopped and pointed out an open area with a partially carved totem pole. "When I came here for vacation for the first time at the age of thirteen, I used to sit here and watch the local Indians carve the totem poles. When you told me about the ones in the entranceway to your house and where they came from, I had this gut feeling Victoria would connect our lives somehow."

As they peddled past the front of the Parliament Buildings and into James Bay, Michael lead them up Douglas Street to Beacon Hill Park. As they got to Dallas Road, Michael pointed out the mile marker sign. They were at the farthest point in North America.

Michael turned left on Cambridge Street where he parked his bike in front of the third house from Dallas Road. He turned to Felicia and pointed. "This is where my Aunt and Uncle lived. If only I had known how untouchable real estate would become, I would've brought this house."

They headed back out onto Dallas road and drove along the ocean. The Cascade Mountain Range reached high into the clouds across the Straits of Juan De Fuca. As they peddled past the shipyard and around the tip of James Bay, Michael turned onto Quebec Street. He stopped in front of an apartment building and pointed up to the third-floor balcony. "That was where my grandmother lived." He then pulled the bike around to the back and showed Felicia the corner unit. "That was my first apartment."

They were both feeling hungry and Michael suggested going to a pizzeria he used to frequent. They biked down Government Street to Market Square. It was still there.

"I used to order a whole wheat pizza with celery and pepperoni, absolutely delicious." He told her. They went inside and Michael turned Felicia on to something she had never had before. "Goodness, hon, this is the best pizza besides our homemade ones I have ever tasted." Michael agreed. After lunch they headed up Yates Street looking for the old book store.

Victoria had experienced an influx of new venture capitalists who rebuilt the once quaint English city into rows of cafes and bistros and artsy businesses much like the ones Amanda spoke about when she lived in Soho. There it was after all these years. *"Treasures Book Shop."*

He parked his bike took Felicia by the hand and led her inside.

An older man was sitting behind the counter and rose up to greet them as they walked in. "Welcome friends, if you need anything, just ask, after forty-seven years, I am quite certain I know where everything is."

His face lit up as he looked out over his half-rimmed spectacles at Michael and Felicia, he took a step back, affixed his eyes on Michael and scratched his head as if, he had seen him somewhere in time.

As they strolled through the aisles, Felicia couldn't help but reminisce and admire how organized and detailed each shelf was. There were thousands of books, all labeled and in alphabetical order. As she panned a row of books on Eastern meditation, she felt something tingling inside and thought to herself. *"There is something about this place that washes through me like a cleansing of my entire being. I have been here many times growing up in Oak Bay, but this time is special, like a spiritual calling."*

As she opened the book began glancing through the pages, Michael walked to the back of the shop.

As he panned the wall filled with framed historical pieces and prints, his eyes fell upon the one piece he had treasured for years. He stood in front of what appeared to be the connection he brought Felicia to Victoria in the first place for, the old man walked up beside him. Before he could say anything, Michael reached up and took the framed work in his hands and walked it over to Felicia. The old man followed.

As he handed it to her, he put his hands on her face, kissed her and said. "I never said anything the day I saw this because I wanted to take you where it all began. I've known all along there was a divine connection between us. That day in your office, I discovered what is was."

The old man looked over at the piece Michael had given Felicia and without saying a word smiled as he remembered after all these years, who this man was.

Felicia took one look at the framed writing and burst into tears. There it was staring back at her. The divine connection that she felt washing through her. She began to read it to Michael as he wiped the tears from her face.

"Wind swept sea,
Sand castles and memories.
So much I have seen through these pale blue skies,
I often wonder, if only, I could fly.
Far away lies the end, a still, quiet mystery,
Horizons begin there where my eyes meet the sea.
A grain of sand where once stood a sand castle,
It's all in the wind now, it's all in the wind now."
Written by: The Poetry Man

She looked up, placed the frame up against her chest smiled, shook her head and said. "So, Michael, you are The Poetry Man."

"Yes, the old man said. "Michael Langston is, The Poetry Man."

Conclusion

Felicia Stouffer and Michael Langston married as planned in mid-July.

Michael's inclination was right that they would find a location on the Island to hold their wedding. During their stay in Victoria, they toured Butchart Gardens in Brentwood Bay and fell in love with the Sunken Garden. While they were there, Michael and Felicia toured the surrounding area looking at lake front building lots.

They exchanged their nuptials atop the rock mound in the center of the garden as their guests observed from below forming a circle around the mount and holding hands as the vows were read.

The idea to do this was presented by Amanda Turner, the artist who designed the book cover for Michael's novella as well as the dress and accessories Felicia wore on her wedding day.

She was a certified yoga practitioner and believed in one's ability to send or radiate love from within, outward. She handed each guest a small card with the words, *"I am sending you the energy of love to have and to hold today and for all the days of your life."* This was said in unison as Felicia and Michael accepted one another's love and became united as husband and wife.

Felicia looked absolutely, breathtaking in her Bohemian styled beaded applique, lace dress accented by a flowered head band and wristlet. Michael wore a white linen suit with an emerald green paisley vest and button down, white silk shirt.

They stood barefoot as they read their vows atop the rock mount and ascended as Mr. and Mrs. Langston to the tune of, "You Are So Beautiful."

The reception took place in the Rose Garden. One long table similar, to the theme at Cal and Candice's wedding was set up to accommodate the bride and groom and thirty- two guests which included Jerry and Manning Bristol who flew in from England as promised. The kitchen staff at the Gardens prepared a fabulous dining experience. It was as Felicia and Michael wanted it, simple but elegant, surrounded by nature's beauty.

The newlyweds drove back to Seattle stopping in Sequim Valley to attend the annual lavender festival. For their honeymoon, they flew from Seattle to the Philippines where they kayaked an underground river, went rock climbing and explored remote villages to gather information on missionary opportunities.

Arriving back in San Francisco presented a whole new life for Mr. and Mrs. Langston. Michael had given his apartment up to Amanda. She mentioned being interested in it if he ever moved out, so it worked out perfectly. One of the perks she offered Michael was free painting lessons which he eagerly accepted.

Michael was now residing with his bride in the Sausalito home he stayed in as a guest upon his arrival in California.

"Manning Osborne of Kingstanding," was published under Felicia's and Michael's new publishing house, "**FaMiLy**," which represented their initials and purpose to provide for children as they originally discussed.

The coming months were filled with the excitement of the book garnering the attention of some very influential people as a result of Felicia's marketing savvy. Within three months over one hundred thousand copies had been sold making it to the New York Times best seller list. Once it made that prestigious list, screenwriters began expressing an interest in doing a movie and talk shows wanted the up and coming author as a guest.

For all requests, Michael was self-represented and would respond. "My publicist is part of the package, so if you want me, she gets included and I say that because she is also my wife and partner in this dream-come-true. He would then add. "Once you hear about our future plans and aspirations together, we, make for an even more interesting story than me alone."

And they did appear and talked about not only helping aspiring writers but about the missionary work and their foundation, viewers responded by flooding the stations with calls asking how they could get involved.

Outsiders might say it was a one hit wonder, a fluke or just that the writer had connections. but the fact was, not only was the story about Manning Osborne's life a damn good book based on an actual event that took place and, was superbly written, the Langston's had a divine purpose, a worthwhile mission for everything they were undertaking. As for a one hit wonder, that was only the beginning for Michael Langston. The author had amassed enough material over his forty years of writing to pen at least three more books.

As the sales revenues from the book started coming in, Felicia and Michael began setting the stage for their dream of helping children. Their first donation would go to the children's hospital where Manning worked after all, that is where this whole dream began to unfold. When they wrote out the first check for twenty thousand dollars, Felicia and Michael looked at one another and cried tears of happiness.

Two years had passed since Felicia and Michael married.

They continued working. Felicia still played an integral part at 21st Century Advertising while Michael stayed on at The Plymouth Rock Inn. Although he was now becoming a prolific literary personality, Michael used his time at the inn to help Dana's business reach new heights.

He would do book signings and hold writing workshops for aspiring writers in turn, the inn generated a new type of cash flow. All proceeds from book signings would go to the foundation while the fees charged for the writer's workshops would go directly to Dana for hosting the events. It was a win, win situation for all involved.

If Michael discovered a writer, he felt had the talent to be published, he would entertain their manuscript and pass it along to Felicia.

She trusted Michael's recommendations and would undertake the editing process.

Amanda Turner would design the cover and Ingrid Olson would complete the process of getting the book's proof copy printed. This was all part of Michael's workshop fee which, was a very smart marketing tactic. Every writer wants to be able to hold in their hands a physical copy of their book and the workshop gave them that opportunity.

Not all writer's material would sell, like a painter who creates a canvas of art, not every painter will have their works hung in galleries. But for a writer or an artist there is the gratification of producing something tangible. Michael saw that in his own paintings as he progressed with Amanda's teaching. It wasn't so much an aspiration to hang his art in MOMA as it was the satisfaction of applying color to a canvas, simple.

Two years after it hit the shelves, Michael's first book was still receiving attention all due to a recent article talking about it being made into a movie and who would be best cast in the main characters role.

He had since penned a motivational book with daily affirmations which was a whole different genre and audience and a children's book about a unicorn. These books had to reach a whole different audience and sales were sluggish. They did sell once people could detach themselves from the expectations that had for a book that would follow the theme of a Manning Osborne type of story. In his heart, "The Poetry Man", knew it was time to put another real good story out there and he knew exactly where that story would come from.

As he and Felicia were sitting out on the deck sipping their wine and enjoying a star lit sky, Michael offered up something that has been going through his head for months. "Honey, are you ready to move on?"

Felicia went to respond as if to question what he meant by that but stopped and thought about what he had just asked. "If you are talking about moving on to the next phase of our life, yes, I am." She replied.

Michael went on. "I think you can honestly say, you have reached the utmost pinnacle of success in your career. I am talking about advertising not our publishing company, that is a whole new beginning for both of us and the beautiful thing about this honey is we can take it wherever we go. We have the wind at our backs right now let's fly."

"My darling, you and I have made one another young again, that in the coming years, we will never exhaust our ability to think, feel and stay...as if I remember it. Michael stopped. "Wait, I have it right here in my wallet." He pulled out a small piece of paper, unfolded it and began to read:

"I told her that I felt like a twenty-year-old again. That this man and I are in our fifties and it feels like time stood still wherever we were in our lives back then, catapulted us through what we have both gone through in getting to where we are today and then took us back in time to meet and fall in love."

'So, there it is my love, the words that define you and I as a couple and how we enhance one another."

Michael took Felicia's hand and led her to the balcony.

"See those stars up there?" Look for the two brightest ones and you will see you and me. Next to those stars is the light that makes us shine. As, long as, we can see the light, we can do whatever we dream and that is the most beautiful thing about our love, that light will never fade, those stars will always shine brightly, and our dreams will never die."

The End.......

About the Author

Rich Osborne has been writing since he was eight years old. Born with a sixty-five percent hearing loss in both ears, imagery and the ability to capture those images in words enabled him to describe what he was feeling. Nature became his escape from the hearing world, and he began writing poems to describe his feelings about the beauty he saw. His grandmother enhanced his ability to write by introducing him to the world of reading at the age of two at the public library.

As he got older, he questioned her about his uncanny ability to so eloquently capture the world he not only witnessed but envisioned, a world of being at peace with nature. She simply replied. "You have a gift that has been passed down through the generations, generations of biblical scholars, writers, artists, thespians and educators and because you submerged yourself in great literary works from a young age, you were able to develop your own style of expression."

The author used that gift as a positive tool to motivate others in his first book, "How to Be Positive, Manifesting Your Dreams and Discovering Your True Self." His second book, "Insights" captured the beauty of nature he saw, through the lens of a camera.

His latest novel, "The Poetry Man," has taken the writer in a whole new direction. Writing his first romance novel was quite the undertaking especially when it came to developing characters, and a story that would keep his readers so vividly in tune with the people, places and events, they would feel as if they were sitting in a theater watching an epic love story. The author reflected on some of the issues he faced putting the storyline for this book together. "I have to admit, writing the love scenes was my greatest challenge. I wanted to engage both the female and male reader in scenes that were tasteful and at the same time, romantic. I wanted my readers to inject themselves into the characters and feel their love for one another. After many rewrites and critical reviews of the scenes, I can rest assured, my readers will agree I captured what I set out to accomplish and that was, delicate and classy written love scenes."

A Special Message

This book was penned during one of the most trying times of our lives, the Coronavirus pandemic. Mother nature has a way of unleashing fury as does war and most recently mass shootings. All of these have affected us as a society, but none has had a world impact like COVID-19.

My heartfelt thanks go out to all those frontline heroes and first responders. I am proud to be one of them.

May Bless All of You and Your Loved Ones,

Rich Osborne

Made in the USA
Columbia, SC
01 May 2025